A POCKETFUL OF LAUGHS

Stories, Poems, Jokes & Riddles

Selections from THE LAUGH BOOK

Compiled by
Joanna Cole
and
Stephanie Calmenson

Drawings by
Marylin Hafner

A Doubleday Book for Young Readers

A Doubleday Book for Young Readers
Published by Delacorte Press
Bantam Doubleday Dell Publishing Group, Inc.
1540 Broadway, New York, New York 10036
Doubleday and the portrayal of an anchor with a dolphin are trademarks of Bantam Doubleday Dell Publishing Group, Inc.

RL: 2.5 Art direction by Diana Klemin.
Printed in the United States of America BVG May 1995
ISBN 0–385–32154–6

Published by arrangement with GuildAmerica® Books, an imprint and a registered trademark of Doubleday Book & Music Clubs, Inc.
Dept. GB, 401 Franklin Avenue, Garden City, New York 11530

Acknowledgments

All possible care has been taken to make full acknowledgment in every case where material is still in copyright. If errors have occurred, they will be corrected in subsequent editions if notification is sent to the publisher. Grateful acknowledgment is made for permission to reprint the following:

Harry Allard. *It's So Nice to Have a Wolf Around the House* by Harry Allard, illustrated by James Marshall. Copyright © 1977 by Harry Allard, illustrations copyright © 1977 by James Marshall. Used by permission of Doubleday, a division of Bantam Doubleday Dell Publishing Group, Inc.

Richard Armour. "The Catsup Bottle" from *It All Started with Columbus*, revised edition by Richard Armour. Copyright © 1961 by Richard Armour. Reprinted by permission of Kathleen S. Armour.

Judi Barrett. Adapted excerpt from *Cloudy with a Chance of Meatballs* by Judi Barrett. Text copyright © 1978 by Judi Barrett. Adapted with permission of Atheneum Publishers, an imprint of Macmillan Publishing Company.

Judy Blume. "Dribble!" from *Tales of a Fourth Grade Nothing* by Judy Blume, illustrated by Roy Doty. Text copyright © 1972 by Judy Blume. Illustrations © 1972 by E. P. Dutton. Used by permission of Dutton Children's Books, a division of Penguin Books USA Inc.

Gyles Brandreth. Excerpt from "Oyster Stew" from *The Biggest Tongue Twister Book in the World* by Gyles Brandreth. Text © 1977 by Gyles Brandreth. Copyright © 1978 by Sterling Publishing Co., Inc. Reprinted with permission of Sterling Publishing Co., Inc., 387 Park Ave. S., New York, NY 10016.

Stephanie Calmenson. "Best Sellers" by Stephanie Calmenson. Copyright © 1986 by Stephanie Calmenson. "Row, Row, Row Your Goat" by Stephanie Calmenson from *Never Take a Pig to Lunch* by Stephanie Calmenson. Copyright © 1982 by Stephanie Calmenson. Reprinted by permission of Doubleday, a division of Bantam Doubleday Dell Publishing Group, Inc.

David Allen Clark. Jokes are excerpted from *The Giant Joke Book* by David Allen Clark. Copyright © 1981 by Doubleday & Company, Inc. Reprinted by permission of the publisher.

Beverly Cleary. Text of "Otis Takes Aim" and illustrations in *Otis Spofford* by Beverly Cleary. Text copyright 1953 by Beverly Cleary. By permission of Morrow Junior Books, a division of William Morrow & Company, Inc.

Joanna Cole. "Hippopotamus" is copyright © 1982 by Joanna Cole.

William Cole. "Knock, Knock Jokes" from *Knock Knocks You've Never Heard Before* by William Cole. Copyright © 1977 by William Cole. "Puzzling" by William Cole from *An Arkful of Animals* selected by William Cole. Copyright © 1978 by William Cole. Reprinted by permission of the author.

Roald Dahl. "The Funny Walking Stick," "Mrs. Twit Has the Shrinks" and "Mrs. Twit Gets a Shrinking" from *The Twits* by Roald Dahl. Copyright © 1980 by Roald Dahl. Reprinted by permission of Alfred A. Knopf, Inc.

Milton Drake, Al Hoffman and Jerry Livingston. "Mairzy Doats" by Al Hoffman, Milton Drake and Jerry Livingston. Copyright 1943 (Renewed) by Al Hoffman Songs, Inc. (ASCAP), Hallmark Music Co., and Drake Activities Corporation. International Copyright Secured. All Rights Reserved. Reprinted by permission.

Madeleine Edmondson. "Two Elephants" by Madeleine Edmondson. Copyright © 1986 by Madeleine Edmondson. Reprinted by permission of the author.

Delia Ephron. "How to Get a Dog" from *How to Eat Like a Child* by Delia Ephron, illustrated by Edward Koren. Copyright © 1977, 1978 by Delia Ephron; illustrations copyright © 1978 by Edward Koren. Used by permission of Viking Penguin, a division of Penguin Books USA Inc.

Charles Keller. "Newsbreaks" from *Newsbreaks* by Charles Keller. Copyright © 1980 by Charles Keller. Reprinted by permission of the author.

Stephen Manes. "The Boy Who Turned into a TV Set" from *The Boy Who Turned into a TV Set* by Stephen Manes, illustrated by Michael Bass. Text copyright © 1979 by Stephen Manes. Illustrations copyright © 1979 by Michael Bass. Text reprinted by permission of the author. Illustrations by Michael Bass reprinted by permission of Putnam & Grosset Group.

Ogden Nash. "The Ostrich" (from "Nature Walks") from *Verses from 1929 On* by Ogden Nash. Copyright © 1956 by Ogden Nash. Copyright © renewed 1984 by Frances Nash, Isabel Nash Eberstadt, and Linell Nash Smith. By permission of Little, Brown and Company. "Celery" from *Verses from 1929 On* by Ogden Nash. Copyright 1941 by Ogden Nash. By permission of Little, Brown and Company.

Peggy Parish. Entire text of *Amelia Bedelia* by Peggy Parish and eleven specified illustrations by Fritz Siebel. Text copyright © 1963 by Margaret Parish. Pictures copyright © 1963 by Fritz Siebel. Reprinted by permission of HarperCollins Publishers.

Pat Relf. The text of "How to Be the Perfect Host" is derived from *Muppet Manners (or The Night Gonzo Gave a Party)*. Copyright © 1981 by Jim Henson Productions, Inc. All rights reserved. Reprinted by permission of Jim Henson Productions, Inc.

Thomas Rockwell. "The First Worm" from *How to Eat Fried Worms* by Thomas Rockwell. Text copyright © 1973 by Thomas Rockwell. Reprinted by arrangement with Orchard Books, New York.

Susan Alton Schmeltz. "Never Take a Pig to Lunch" by Susan Alton Schmeltz appeared originally in *Cricket* Magazine, January 1977. Copyright © 1977 by Susan M. Schmeltz. Reprinted by permission of the author.

Charles M. Schulz. Cartoon "The Doctor Is In" by Charles M. Schulz. © 1968 United Feature Syndicate, Inc. By permission of UFS, Inc.

Barbara Seuling. "You Can't Eat Peanuts in Church and Other Little-known Laws" from *You Can't Eat Peanuts in Church and Other Little-known Laws* by Barbara Seuling. Copyright © 1975 by Barbara Seuling. Reprinted by permission of Russell & Volkening as agents for the author.

Shel Silverstein. "Boa Constrictor" from *Where the Sidewalk Ends: The Poems and Drawings of Shel Silverstein*. Copyright © 1974 by Snake Eye Music, Inc. Reprinted by permission of HarperCollins Publishers.

Isaac Bashevis Singer. "The First Shlemiel" from *Zlateh the Goat and Other Stories* by Isaac Bashevis Singer. Translated from Yiddish by Isaac Bashevis Singer and Elizabeth Shub. Illustrated by Maurice Sendak. Text copyright © 1966 by Isaac Bashevis Singer. Pictures copyright © 1966 by Maurice Sendak. Reprinted by permission of HarperCollins Publishers.

Mike Thaler. "The Frog Speaker" from *The Yellow Brick Toad* by Mike Thaler. Copyright © 1978 by Mike Thaler. Reprinted by permission of Andrea Brown Literary Agency, Inc.

Bernard Wiseman. "The Tongue-Twister" from "Morris and Boris and the Tongue Twister" in *Morris and Boris: Three Stories* by Bernard Wiseman. Copyright © 1974 by Bernard Wiseman. Reprinted by permission of the author.

Contents

• 4 •

Last Laughs

137

Introduction

We know that no kid ever reads
an introduction.
So we're just going to skip it.

1

Funny Stories

The First Worm

by Thomas Rockwell

Would you eat fifteen worms to win a fifty-dollar bet? Billy wants to buy a minibike so badly, he's going to try. With his pal, Tom, as his coach, Billy tackles the first worm served by opponents Alan and Joe.

The huge night crawler sprawled limply in the center of the platter, brown and steaming.

"Boiled," said Tom. "We boiled it."

Billy stormed about the barn, kicking barrels and posts, arguing. "A night crawler isn't a *worm!* If it was a worm, it'd be called a worm. A night crawler's a night crawler."

Finally Joe ran off to get his father's dictionary:

> **night crawler** *n:* EARTHWORM; *esp:* a large earthworm found on the soil surface at night

Billy kicked a barrel. It still wasn't fair; he didn't care what any dictionary said; everybody knew the difference between a night crawler and a worm—look at the thing. Yergh! It was as big as a souvenir pencil from the Empire State Building! Yugh! He poked it with his finger.

"You can't quit now," said Tom. "Look at them." He nodded at Alan and Joe, waiting beside the orange crates. "They'll tell everybody you were chicken. It'll be all over school. Come on."

He led Billy back to the orange crates, sat him down, tied the napkin around his neck.

Alan flourished the knife and fork.

"Would monshure like eet carved lingthvise or cruss-vise?"

"Kitchip?" asked Joe, showing his teeth.

"Cut it out," said Tom. "Here." He glopped ketchup and mustard and horseradish on the night crawler, squeezed on a few drops of lemon juice, and salted and peppered it.

Billy closed his eyes and opened his mouth. "Ou woot in."

Tom sliced off the end of the night crawler and forked it up. But just as he was about to poke it into Billy's open mouth, Billy closed his mouth and opened his eyes. "No, let me do it."

Tom handed him the fork. Billy gazed at the dripping ketchup and mustard, thinking, Awrgh! It's all right talking about eating worms, but *doing* it!?!

Tom whispered in his ear. "Minibike."

"Glug." Billy poked the fork into his mouth, chewed furiously, *gulped! . . . gulped! . . .* His eyes crossed, swam, squinched shut. He flapped his arms wildly. And then, opening his eyes, he grinned beatifically up at Tom.

"Superb, Gaston."

Tom cut another piece, ketchuped, mustarded, salted, peppered, horseradished, and lemoned it, and handed the fork to Billy. Billy slugged it down, smacking his lips. And so they proceeded, now sprinkling on cinnamon and sugar or a bit of cheese, some cracker crumbs or Worcestershire sauce, until there was nothing on the plate but a few stray dabs of ketchup and mustard.

"Vell," said Billy, standing up and wiping his mouth with his napkin. "So. Ve are done mit de first curse. Naw seconds?"

"Lemme look in your mouth," said Alan.

"Yeah," said Joe. "See if he swallowed it all."

"Soitinly, soitinly," said Billy. "Luke as long as you vant."

Alan and Joe scrutinized the inside of his mouth.

"Okay, okay," said Tom. "Leave him alone now. Come on. One down, fourteen to go."

"How'd it taste?" asked Alan.

"Gute, gute," said Billy. "Ver'fine, ver'fine. Hoo hoo." He flapped his arms like a big bird and began to hop around the barn, crying, "Gute, gute. Ver'fine, ver'fine. Gute, gute."

Alan and Joe and Tom looked worried.

"Uh, yeah—gute, gute. How you feeling, Billy?" Tom asked.

"Yeah, stop flapping around and come tell us how you're feeling," said Joe.

They huddled together by the orange crates as Billy hopped around and around them, flapping his arms.

"Gute, gute. Ver'fine, ver'fine. Hoo hoo."

Alan whispered, "He's crackers."

Joe edged toward the door. "Don't let him see we're afraid. Crazy people are like dogs. If they see you're afraid, they'll attack."

"It couldn't *be,"* whispered Tom, standing his ground. "One worm?"

"Gute, gute," screeched Billy, hopping higher and higher and drooling from the mouth.

"Come *on,"* whispered Joe to Tom.

"Hey, *Billy!"* burst out Tom suddenly in a hearty, quavering voice. "Cut it out, will you? I want to ask you something."

Billy's arms flapped slower. He tiptoed menacingly around Tom, his head cocked on one side, his cheeks puffed out. Tom hugged himself, chuckling nervously.

"Heh, heh. Cut it out, will you, Billy? Heh, heh."

Billy pounced. Joe and Alan fled, the barn door banging behind them. Billy rolled on the floor, helpless with laughter.

Tom clambered up, brushing himself off.

"Did you see their *faces?"* Billy said, laughing. "Climbing over each other out the door? Oh! Geez! Joe was pale as an onion."

"Yeah," said Tom. "Ha, ha. You fooled them."

"Ho! Geez!" Billy sat up. Then he crawled over to the door and peered out through a knothole. "Look at them, peeking up over the stone wall. Watch this."

The door swung slowly open.

Screeching, Billy hopped onto the doorsill!—into the yard!—up onto a stump!—splash into a puddle!—flapping his arms, rolling his head.

Alan and Joe galloped up the hill through the high grass, yelling, "Here he comes! Get out of the way!"

And then Billy stopped hopping, and climbing up on the stump, called in a shrill, girlish voice, "Oh, boy-oys, where are you go-ing? Id somefing tare you, iddle boys?"

Alan and Joe stopped and looked back.

"Id oo doughing home, iddle boys?" yelled Billy. "Id oo tared?"

"Who's scared, you lunk?" called Alan.

"Yeah," yelled Joe. "I guess I can go home without being called scared, if I want to."

"But ain't oo in a dawful hur-ry?" shouted Billy.

"I just remembered I was supposed to help my mother wash windows this afternoon," said Alan. "That's all." He turned and started up through the meadow, his hands in his pockets.

"Yeah," said Joe. "Me, too." He trudged after Alan.

It's So Nice to Have a Wolf Around the House

by Harry Allard
Illustrated by James Marshall

Once upon a time there was an old man who lived alone with his three old pets. There was his dog Peppy, who was very old. There was his cat Ginger, who was very, very old. And there was Lightning, his tropical fish, who was so old that she could barely swim and preferred to float.

One day the Old Man called his three pets together and said to them, "The trouble, my friends, is that we are all so very old." Peppy wagged his tail in agreement, but just barely; Ginger twitched her ears in agreement, but just barely; and Lightning waved her fin but fell over backward because of the effort involved.

"What we need," the Old Man continued, "is a charming companion—someone to take care of us and pep us up." Lightning and Ginger and Peppy thought the Old Man was right. But this time they were too tired to wag, twitch, or wave in agreement.

That very day the Old Man put an ad in the newspaper: *Wanted: A charming companion.* [Signed] *The Old Man.*

Early the next morning a furry stranger knocked on the Old Man's door. He had long white teeth and long black nails. Handing the old man an engraved visiting card, he introduced himself. "Cuthbert Q. Devine, at your service," he said, tipping his hat. "Did you advertise for a charming companion, Old Man?"

"Yes I did," the Old Man said.

"Look no further! I am the very one you have been searching for." Cuthbert smiled from ear to ear. "Many people think that I am a wolf. That, of course, is nonsense, utter nonsense. As a matter of fact, I happen to be a dog—a German shepherd to be exact." And Cuthbert laughed in a deep, wolfish voice.

The Old Man was completely dazzled by Cuthbert Q. Devine's charming personality. He particularly liked his big bright smile. And because the Old Man's eyesight was not what it used to be, he did not see Cuthbert for what he really was—a wolf!

"You're hired," the Old Man said. And Cuthbert Q. Devine moved in, bag and baggage.

Cuthbert had not been on the job twenty-four hours before the Old Man and his three pets wondered how they had ever managed without him. First up and last to bed, Cuthbert cleaned and cooked and paid the bills. He took Peppy for long walks. He groomed Ginger and introduced her to the use of catnip. He fixed up Lightning's aquarium. He was a whiz at making fancy desserts. He massaged the Old Man's toes. He played the viola. And every Saturday night he organized a fancy costume party.

If the Old Man had ever had any doubts about Cuthbert, they were all gone now. Cuthbert had a heart of gold. All he wanted to do was to make the Old Man and his three pets happy.

But it was all too good to last.

Late one afternoon, after Cuthbert had tucked him into his easy chair and handed him his paper, the Old Man read a terrible thing right on page one: *Wanted for Bank Robbery,* the headline said. There was a picture of a wolf in a prison uniform. It was Cuthbert! The Old Man could not believe his eyes.

"To think I hired him as a charming companion, and he was a wolf the whole time!" The Old Man could not get over it. He was hurt . . . and frightened, too.

Pale and shaking, the Old Man confronted Cuthbert in the kitchen. He waved the newspaper in Cuthbert's face. "And you told me you were a German shepherd," he said.

Cuthbert's spoon clattered to the kitchen floor.

"I'm no good," he sobbed. "No good at all. But I can't help it—I've never had a chance. I always wanted to be good, but everyone expected me to be bad because I'm a wolf."

And before the Old Man could say another word, Cuthbert fainted dead away.

Somehow Ginger and Peppy and the Old Man managed to drag Cuthbert to his bed. When the doctor arrived, he said that Cuthbert had had a bad attack of nerves and would have to stay in bed for months if he were ever to get well again. "You've got a very sick wolf on your hands," the doctor told the Old Man as he left.

Now it was the Old Man who got up early to clean and cook and pay the bills. But he did not mind at all—in fact he felt years younger. Peppy helped, and so did Ginger.

With so much to do for Cuthbert, Peppy forgot his aches and pains; and everyone said that Ginger was as frisky as a kitten again. Lightning did her share, too: She spent her days blowing beautiful bubbles to amuse Cuthbert—it seemed to soothe his frayed nerves.

Cuthbert had to stay in bed for a long time, but at last he was well enough to get up. One day he told the Old Man how ashamed he was of robbing all those banks. He asked the Old Man what he should do.

On the Old Man's advice, Cuthbert turned himself in to the police. When his case came to court, Cuthbert promised the judge that he would never rob a bank again. The judge believed him and said, "I will let you go this time because you have done so much for the Old Man and his pets."

The Old Man was very happy. So was Cuthbert, and his paws shook from relief.

Cuthbert finally got completely well and lived with the Old Man and his three pets for the rest of their lives. As a matter of fact, all five of them are still living in Arizona to this day. The Old Man moved there with Lightning and Ginger and Peppy because the desert climate was better for Cuthbert's health.

The Twits

by Roald Dahl

How would you like to finish your milk one day and find a glass eye staring up at you? Or maybe you'd prefer a Giant Skillywiggler in your bed or a juicy surprise in your spaghetti. Those are just a few of the wicked tricks the world's most horrible couple have played on each other. Here is one more you won't forget.

The Funny Walking Stick

To pay Mrs. Twit back for the worms in his spaghetti, Mr. Twit thought up a really clever nasty trick.

One night, when the old woman was asleep, he crept out of bed and took her walking stick downstairs to his workshed. There he stuck a tiny round piece of wood (no thicker than a penny) onto the bottom of the stick.

This made the stick longer, but the difference was so small, the next morning Mrs. Twit didn't notice it.

The following night, Mr. Twit stuck on another tiny bit of wood. Every night, he crept downstairs and added an extra tiny thickness of wood to the end of the walking stick. He did it very neatly so that the extra bits looked like a part of the old stick.

Gradually, but oh so gradually, Mrs. Twit's walking stick was getting longer and longer.

Now, when something is growing very very slowly, it is almost impossible to notice it happening. You yourself, for example, are actually growing taller every day that goes by, but you wouldn't think it, would you? It's happening so slowly you can't even notice it from one week to the next.

It was the same with Mrs. Twit's walking stick. It was all so slow and gradual that she didn't notice how long it was getting even when it was halfway up to her shoulder.

"That stick's too long for you," Mr. Twit said to her one day.

"Why so it is!" Mrs. Twit said, looking at the stick. "I've had a feeling there was something wrong, but I couldn't for the life of me think what it was."

"There's something wrong all right," Mr. Twit said, beginning to enjoy himself.

"What *can* have happened?" Mrs. Twit said, staring at her old walking stick. "It must suddenly have grown longer."

"Don't be a fool!" Mr. Twit said. "How can a walking stick possibly grow longer? It's made of dead wood, isn't it? Dead wood can't grow."

"Then what on earth has happened?" cried Mrs. Twit.

"It's not the stick, it's *you!*" said Mr. Twit, grinning horribly. "It's *you* that's getting *shorter!* I've been noticing it for some time now."

"That's not true!" cried Mrs. Twit.

"You're shrinking, woman!" said Mr. Twit.

"It's not possible!"

"Oh yes it jolly well is," said Mr. Twit. "You're shrinking fast! You're shrinking *dangerously* fast! Why, you must have shrunk at least a foot in the last few days!"

"Never!" she cried.

"Of course you have! Take a look at your stick, you old goat, and see how much you've shrunk in comparison! You've got the *shrinks,* that's what you've got! You've got the dreaded *shrinks!*"

Mr. Twit put on a very solemn face. "At the rate you're going," he said, shaking his head sadly, "I'd say not more than ten or eleven days."

"But isn't there *anything* we can do?" cried Mrs. Twit.

"There's only one cure for the shrinks," said Mr. Twit.

"Tell me!" she cried. "Oh, tell me quickly!"

"We'll have to hurry!" said Mr. Twit.

"I'm ready. I'll hurry! I'll do anything you say!" cried Mrs. Twit.

"You won't last long if you don't," said Mr. Twit, giving her another grizzly grin.

"What is it I must do?" cried Mrs. Twit, clutching her cheeks.

"You've got to be *stretched,*" said Mr. Twit.

Mrs. Twit began to feel so trembly she had to sit down.

As soon as Mrs. Twit sat down, Mr. Twit pointed at her and shouted, "There you are! You're sitting in your old chair and you've shrunk so much your feet aren't even touching the ground!"

Mrs. Twit looked down at her feet and by golly the man was right. Her feet were not touching the ground.

Mr. Twit, you see, had been just as clever with the chair as he'd been with the walking stick. Every night when he had gone downstairs and stuck a little bit extra onto the stick, he had done the same to the four legs of Mrs. Twit's chair.

"Just look at you sitting there in your same old chair," he cried, "and you've shrunk so much your feet are dangling in the air!"

Mrs. Twit went white with fear.

"You've got the *shrinks!*" cried Mr. Twit, pointing his finger at her like a pistol. "You've got them badly! You've got the most terrible case of shrinks I've ever seen!"

Mrs. Twit became so frightened she began to dribble. But Mr. Twit, still remembering the worms in his spaghetti, didn't feel sorry for her at all. "I suppose you know what *happens* to you when you get the shrinks?" he said.

"What?" gasped Mrs. Twit. "What happens?"

"Your head SHRINKS into your neck . . .

"And your neck SHRINKS into your body . . .

"And your body SHRINKS into your legs . . .

"And your legs SHRINK into your feet. And in the end there's nothing left except a pair of shoes and a bundle of old clothes."

"I can't bear it!" cried Mrs. Twit.

"It's a terrible disease," said Mr. Twit. "The worst in the world."

"How long have I got?" cried Mrs. Twit. "How long before I finish up as a bundle of old clothes and a pair of shoes?"

BALLOO

Mr. Twit led Mrs. Twit outdoors, where he had everything ready for the great stretching.

He had one hundred balloons and lots of string.

He had a gas cylinder for filling the balloons.

He had fixed an iron ring into the ground.

"Stand here," he said, pointing to the iron ring. He then tied Mrs. Twit's ankles to the iron ring.

When that was done, he began filling the balloons with gas. Each balloon was on a long string and when it was filled with gas it pulled on its string, trying to go up and up. Mr. Twit tied the ends of the strings to the top half of Mrs. Twit's body. Some he tied around her neck, some under her arms, some to her wrists, and some even to her hair.

Soon there were fifty colored balloons floating in the air above Mrs. Twit's head.

"Can you feel them stretching you?" asked Mr. Twit.

"I can! I can!" cried Mrs. Twit. "They're stretching me like mad."

He put on another ten balloons. The upward pull became very strong.

Mrs. Twit was quite helpless now. With her feet tied to the ground and her arms pulled upward by the balloons, she was unable to move. She was a prisoner, and Mr. Twit had intended to go away and leave her like that for a couple of days and nights to teach her a lesson. In fact, he was just about to leave when Mrs. Twit opened her big mouth and said something silly.

"Are you sure my feet are tied properly to the ground?" she gasped. "If those strings around my ankles break, it'll be goodbye for me!"

And that's what gave Mr. Twit his second nasty idea . . .

THE FIRST SHLEMIEL

by Isaac Bashevis Singer
Illustrated by Maurice Sendak

What is a shlemiel? A shlemiel is a simpleton. A shlemiel is a misfit and a nitwit. A shlemiel is lazy and clumsy too. Here is the original shlemiel.

There are many shlemiels in the world, but the very first one came from the village of Chelm. He had a wife, Mrs. Shlemiel, and a child, Little Shlemiel, but he could not provide for them. His wife used to get up early in the morning to sell vegetables in the marketplace. Mr. Shlemiel stayed at home and rocked the baby to sleep. He also took care of the rooster which lived in the room with them, feeding it corn and water.

Mrs. Shlemiel knew that her husband was unhandy and lazy. He also loved to sleep and had a sweet tooth. It so happened that one night she prepared a potful of delicious jam. The next day she worried that while she was away at the market, her husband would eat it all up. So before she left, she said to him, "Shlemiel, I'm going to the market and I will be back in the evening. There are three things that I want to tell you. Each one is very important."

"What are they?" asked Shlemiel.

"First, make sure that the baby does not fall out of his cradle."

"Good. I will take care of the baby."

"Secondly, don't let the rooster get out of the house."

"Good. The rooster won't get out of the house."

"Thirdly, there is a potful of poison on the shelf. Be careful not to eat it, or you will die," said Mrs. Shlemiel, pointing to the pot of jam she had placed high up in the cupboard.

She had decided to fool him, because she knew that once he tasted the delicious jam, he would not stop eating until the pot was empty. It was just before Hanuk-

kah, and she needed the jam to serve with the holiday pancakes.

As soon as his wife left, Shlemiel began to rock the baby and to sing him a lullaby:

I am a big Shlemiel.
You are a little Shlemiel.
When you grow up,
You will be a big Shlemiel
And I will be an old Shlemiel.
When you have children,
You will be a papa Shlemiel
And I will be a grandpa Shlemiel.

The baby soon fell asleep and Shlemiel dozed too, still rocking the cradle with his foot.

Shlemiel dreamed that he had become the richest man in Chelm. He was so rich that he could eat pancakes with jam not only on Hanukkah but every day of the year. He spent all day with the other wealthy men of Chelm playing games with a golden dreidel. Shlemiel knew a trick, and whenever it was his turn to spin the dreidel, it fell on the winning "G." He grew so famous that nobles from distant countries came to him and said, "Shlemiel, we want you to be our king."

Shlemiel told them he did not want to be a king. But the nobles fell on their knees before him and insisted until he had to agree. They placed a crown on his head and led him to a golden throne. Mrs. Shlemiel, now a queen, no longer needed to sell vegetables in the market. She sat next to him, and between them they shared a huge pancake spread with jam. He ate from one side and she from the other until their mouths met.

As Shlemiel sat and dreamed his sweet dream the rooster suddenly started crowing. It had a very strong voice. When it came out with a cock-a-doodle-doo, it rang like a bell. Now when a bell rang in Chelm, it usually meant there was a fire. Shlemiel awakened from his dream and jumped up in fright, overturning the cradle. The baby fell out and hurt his head. In his confusion Shlemiel ran to the window and opened it to see where the fire was. The moment he opened the window, the excited rooster flew out and hopped away.

Shlemiel called after it, "Rooster, you come back. If Mrs. Shlemiel finds you gone, she will rave and rant and I will never hear the end of it."

But the rooster paid no attention to Shlemiel. It didn't even look back, and soon it had disappeared from sight.

When Shlemiel realized that there was no fire, he closed the window and went back to the crying baby, who by this time had a big bump on his forehead from the fall. With great effort Shlemiel comforted the baby, righted the cradle, and put him back into it.

Again he began to rock the cradle and sing a song:

In my dream I was a rich Shlemiel
But awake I am a poor Shlemiel.
In my dream I ate pancakes with jam;
Awake I chew bread and onion.
In my dream I was Shlemiel the King
But awake I'm just Shlemiel.

Having finally sung the baby to sleep, Shlemiel began to worry about his troubles. He knew that when his wife returned and found the rooster gone and the baby with a bump on his head, she would be beside herself with anger. Mrs. Shlemiel had a very loud voice, and when she scolded and screamed, poor Shlemiel trembled with fear. Shlemiel could foresee that tonight, when she got home, his wife would be angrier than ever before and would berate him and call him names.

Suddenly Shlemiel said to himself, "What is the sense

of such a life? I'd rather be dead." And he decided to end his life. But how to do it? He then remembered what his wife had told him in the morning about the pot of poison that stood on the shelf. "That's what I will do. I will poison myself. When I'm dead she can revile me as much as she likes. A dead Shlemiel does not hear when he is screamed at."

Shlemiel was a short man and he could not reach the shelf. He got a stool, climbed up on it, took down the pot, and began to eat.

"Oh, the poison tastes sweet," he said to himself. He had heard that some poisons have a bitter taste and others are sweet. "But," he reasoned, "sweet poison is better than bitter," and proceeded to finish up the jam. It tasted so good, he licked the pot clean.

After Shlemiel had finished the pot of poison, he lay down on the bed. He was sure that the poison would soon begin to burn his insides and that he would die. But half an hour passed and then an hour, and Shlemiel lay without a single pain in his belly.

"This poison works very slowly," Shlemiel decided. He was thirsty and wanted a drink of water, but there was no water in the house. In Chelm water had to be fetched from an outside well, and Shlemiel was too lazy to go and get it.

Shlemiel remembered that his wife was saving a bottle of apple cider for the holidays. Apple cider was expensive, but when a man is about to die, what is the point of saving money? Shlemiel got out the bottle of cider and drank it down to the last drop.

Now Shlemiel began to have an ache in his stomach, and he was sure that the poison had begun to work. Convinced that he was about to die, he said to himself, "It's not really so bad to die. With such poison I wouldn't mind dying every day." And he dozed off.

He dreamed again that he was a king. He wore three crowns on his head, one on top of the other. Before him stood three golden pots: one filled with pancakes, one with jam, and one with apple cider. Whenever he soiled his beard with eating, a servant wiped it for him with a napkin.

Mrs. Shlemiel, the queen, sat next to him on her separate throne and said, "Of all the kings who ever ruled in Chelm, you are the greatest. The whole of Chelm pays homage to your wisdom. Fortunate is the queen of such a king. Happy is the prince who has you as a father."

Shlemiel was awakened by the sound of the door creaking open. The room was dark and he heard his wife's screechy voice. "Shlemiel, why didn't you light the lamp?"

"It sounds like my wife, Mrs. Shlemiel," Shlemiel said to himself. "But how is it possible that I hear her voice? I happen to be dead. Or can it be that the poison hasn't worked yet and I am still alive?" He got up, his legs shaking, and saw his wife lighting the lamp.

Suddenly she began to scream at the top of her lungs. "Just look at the baby! He has a bump on his head. Shlemiel, where is the rooster, and who drank the apple cider? Woe is me! He drank up the cider! He lost the rooster and let the baby get a bump on his head. Shlemiel, what have you done?"

"Don't scream, dear wife. I'm about to die. You will soon be a widow."

"Die? Widow? What are you talking about? You look healthy as a horse."

"I've poisoned myself," Shlemiel replied.

"Poisoned? What do you mean?" asked Mrs. Shlemiel.

"I've eaten your potful of poison."

And Shlemiel pointed to the empty pot of jam.

"Poison?" said Mrs. Shlemiel. "That's my pot of jam for Hanukkah."

"But you told me it was poison," Shlemiel insisted.

"You fool," she said. "I did that to keep you from eating it before the holiday. Now you've swallowed the whole potful." And Mrs. Shlemiel burst out crying.

Shlemiel too began to cry, but not from sorrow. He wept tears of joy that he would remain alive. The wailing of the parents woke the baby and he too began to yowl. When the neighbors heard all the crying, they came running and soon all of Chelm knew the story. The good neighbors took pity on the Shlemiels and brought them a fresh pot of jam and another bottle of apple cider. The rooster, which had gotten cold and hungry from wandering around outside, returned by itself and the Shlemiels had a happy holiday after all.

As always in Chelm when an unusual event occurred, the Elders came together to ponder over what had happened. For seven days and seven nights they sat wrinkling their foreheads and tugging at their beards, searching for the true meaning of the incident. At the end the sages all came to the same conclusion: A wife who has a child in the cradle and a rooster to take care of should never lie to her husband and tell him that a pot of jam is a pot of poison, or that a pot of poison is a pot of jam, even if he is lazy, has a sweet tooth, and is a shlemiel besides.

Amelia Bedelia

by Peggy Parish
Illustrated by Fritz Siebel

On the new maid's first day at work, Mr. and Mrs. Rogers have to be away from home. They leave a list of things to do, but what they don't know is that Amelia Bedelia has her own *idea of how to follow directions. Wait until they see!*

"Oh, Amelia Bedelia, your first day of work. And I can't be here. But I made a list for you. You do just what the list says," said Mrs. Rogers. Mrs. Rogers got into the car with Mr. Rogers. They drove away.

"My, what nice folks. I'm going to like working here," said Amelia Bedelia.

Amelia Bedelia went inside. "Such a grand house. These must be rich folks. But I must get to work. Here I stand just looking. And me with a whole list of things to do."

Amelia Bedelia stood there a minute longer. "I think I'll make a surprise for them. I'll make a lemon-meringue pie. I do make good pies."

So Amelia Bedelia went into the kitchen. She put a little of this and a pinch of that into a bowl. She mixed and she rolled. Soon her pie was ready to go into the oven.

"There," said Amelia Bedelia. "That's done. Now let's see what this list says."

Amelia Bedelia read,

CHANGE THE TOWELS IN THE GREEN BATHROOM

Amelia Bedelia found the green bathroom.

"Those towels are very nice. Why change them?" she thought. Then Amelia Bedelia remembered what Mrs. Rogers had said. She must do just what the list told her.

"Well, all right," said Amelia Bedelia.

Amelia Bedelia got some scissors. She snipped a little here and a little there. And she changed those towels.

"There," said Amelia Bedelia. She looked at her list again.

DUST THE FURNITURE.

"Did you ever hear tell of such a silly thing? At my house we undust the furniture. But to each his own way."

Amelia Bedelia took one last look at the bathroom. She saw a big box with the words *Dusting Powder* on it.

"Well, look at that. A special powder to dust with!" exclaimed Amelia Bedelia.

So Amelia Bedelia dusted the furniture.

"That should be dusty enough. My, how nice it smells."

DRAW THE DRAPES WHEN THE SUN COMES IN.

read Amelia Bedelia. She looked up. The sun was coming in. Amelia Bedelia looked at the list again.

"Draw the drapes? That's what it says. I'm not much of a hand at drawing, but I'll try."

So Amelia Bedelia sat right down and she drew those drapes. Amelia Bedelia marked off about the drapes.

"Now what?"

PUT THE LIGHTS OUT WHEN YOU FINISH IN THE LIVING ROOM.

Amelia Bedelia thought about this a minute. She switched off the lights. Then she carefully unscrewed each bulb. And Amelia Bedelia put the lights out.

"So those things need to be aired out, too. Just like pillows and babies. Oh, I do have a lot to learn.

"My pie!" exclaimed Amelia Bedelia. She hurried to the kitchen.

"Just right," she said. She took the pie out of the oven and put it on the table to cool. Then she looked at the list.

MEASURE TWO CUPS OF RICE.

"That's next," said Amelia Bedelia. Amelia Bedelia found two cups. She filled them with rice. And Amelia Bedelia measured that rice.

Amelia Bedelia laughed. "These folks do want me to do funny things." Then she poured the rice back into the container.

THE MEAT MARKET WILL DELIVER A STEAK AND A CHICKEN.

PLEASE TRIM THE FAT BEFORE YOU PUT THE STEAK IN THE ICEBOX.

AND PLEASE DRESS THE CHICKEN.

When the meat arrived, Amelia Bedelia opened the bag. She looked at the steak for a long time.

"Yes," she said. "That will do nicely." Amelia Bedelia got some lace and bits of ribbon. And Amelia Bedelia trimmed that fat before she put the steak in the icebox.

"Now I must dress the chicken. I wonder if she wants a he chicken or a she chicken?" said Amelia Bedelia.

Amelia Bedelia went right to work. Soon the chicken was finished. Amelia Bedelia heard the door open.

"The folks are back," she said. She rushed out to meet them.

"Amelia Bedelia, why are all the light bulbs outside?" asked Mr. Rogers.

"The list just said to put the lights out," said Amelia Bedelia. "It didn't say to bring them back in. Oh, I do hope they didn't get aired too long."

"Amelia Bedelia, the sun will fade the furniture. I asked you to draw the drapes," said Mrs. Rogers.

"I did! I did! See," said Amelia Bedelia. She held up her picture.

Then Mrs. Rogers saw the furniture. "The furniture!" she cried.

"Did I dust it well enough?" asked Amelia Bedelia. "That's such nice dusting powder."

Mr. Rogers went to wash his hands. "I say," he called. "These are very unusual towels."

Mrs. Rogers dashed into the bathroom. "Oh, my best towels," she said.

"Didn't I change them enough?" asked Amelia Bedelia.

Mrs. Rogers went to the kitchen. "I'll cook the dinner. Where is the rice I asked you to measure?"

"I put it back in the container. But I remember—it measured four and a half inches," said Amelia Bedelia.

"Was the meat delivered?" asked Mrs. Rogers.

"Yes," said Amelia Bedelia. "I trimmed the fat just like you said. It does look nice."

Mrs. Rogers rushed to the icebox. She opened it.

"Lace! Ribbons! Oh, dear!" said Mrs. Rogers.

"The chicken—you dressed the chicken?" asked Mrs. Rogers.

"Yes, and I found the nicest box to put him in," said Amelia Bedelia.

"Box!" exclaimed Mrs. Rogers.

Mrs. Rogers hurried over to the box. She lifted the lid. There lay the chicken. And he was just as dressed as he could be.

Mrs. Rogers was angry. She was very angry. She opened her mouth. Mrs. Rogers meant to tell Amelia Bedelia she was fired. But before she could get the words out, Mr. Rogers put something in her mouth. It was so good Mrs. Rogers forgot about being angry.

"Lemon-meringue pie!" she exclaimed.

"I made it to surprise you," said Amelia Bedelia happily. So right then and there Mr. and Mrs. Rogers decided that Amelia Bedelia must stay. And so she did.

Mrs. Rogers learned to say undust the furniture, unlight the lights, close the drapes, and things like that. Mr. Rogers didn't care if Amelia Bedelia trimmed all of his steaks with lace.

All he cared about was having her there to make lemon meringue pie.

The Boy Who Turned into a TV Set

by Stephen Manes

Ogden Pettibone watched television so much that one day he woke up and found that he had turned into one. He had no control over the programming, so he never knew what would come out of his mouth. As you'll see, this can be a problem on a crowded bus . . .

The new television did not sleep well that night. The glow from his screen didn't shine through the covers, but his mouth occasionally fell open as he dozed off, and then a loud commercial or an audience howling at a comedian's joke would waken him.

He was tired and hungry when he came down to breakfast, but his parents asked him not to eat until the commercials came on so that they wouldn't miss any of the morning news. Ogden obliged them, but he did feel rather chilly sitting at the table without a shirt on.

After breakfast, he and his father rode to the doctor's office on a bus. It was crowded, but they found two seats together, and everything was fine until Ogden yawned.

"I hate to be the one to tell you this," a girl's voice said through his mouth, "but you have bad breath."

"WHAT?" stormed the enormous woman beside him. "Who said that?"

"Bad breath," the voice repeated before Ogden could close his jaws.

"I do *not!*" the woman huffed. "I don't know who you think you are, but you had better apologize, sonny!"

Ogden would have liked to, but he knew there was no telling what might come out if he opened his mouth again. He kept it shut.

"Please excuse him," his father told the woman. "I'm sure he didn't mean it."

"Then why did he say it? The least he can do is apologize for himself."

"He really is sorry," said Mr. Pettibone. "Aren't you, Ogden?"

Ogden nodded.

"You didn't mean it, did you?"

Ogden shook his head.

"Humph," the woman sniffed, and turned away.

Just then the bus went over a bump in the road, jolting its passengers so violently that Ogden's jaw dropped open again. "Do you have trouble losing weight?" asked an announcer's voice before Ogden could get himself under control.

The huge woman turned bright red and looked as though she might explode any second. Mr. Pettibone whisked his son to the exit, and marched him off the bus.

"I know it wasn't your fault," Mr. Pettibone told Ogden as they walked toward the doctor's office, "but please try to keep your mouth closed. We wouldn't want another unpleasant incident."

Ogden nodded and clenched his teeth.

The doctor's waiting room was filled with sick kids and their parents. Ogden found a book on airplanes and sat down beside his father to read it.

"My name's Jennifer," said a runny-nosed little girl who came up to him. "What's yours?"

Ogden didn't want to be unfriendly, but he thought he'd better not try to say anything.

"Hey! I said what's your name!"

Ogden just smiled, keeping his lips tight.

"Tell me your name!" the girl insisted, jumping in the air and landing right on Ogden's toes.

Ogden opened his mouth to say "Ow!" but what came out instead was a lionlike roar: "GRRRRRRRRRR!" It sounded so realistic, it scared little Jennifer back to her mother.

"Quite a cough your son has," commented the woman sitting next to Ogden's father. "I certainly hope it isn't contagious." Mr. Pettibone shook his head.

The nurse led Ogden and his father to an examining room. "The doctor will be with you shortly," she told Ogden. "Please take off all your clothes except your underpants."

Ogden did. He checked his screen. It was showing a soap opera, so he didn't bother to open his mouth to listen.

"Hello, Ogden," Doctor Stark said cheerfully when he came in a few minutes later. "What seems to be the trouble?"

Ogden pointed to the picture on his stomach. His father explained the problem.

"Hmmmm," said the doctor, bending over to take a look. "Unusual." He pointed a tongue depressor toward Ogden's mouth. "Say 'ah.' "

Ogden tried. What came out instead was a woman's voice saying, "I'm afraid there's not much hope for Penny after that terrible auto accident."

"Hmmmm," said the doctor again, and peered intently at Ogden's screen.

"Do you think it's serious?" his father asked.

"Oh, Penny will pull through," Doctor Stark reassured him. "She has to. She's the star of the show."

"But what about Ogden?" Mr. Pettibone wondered.

"Hmmmm," said Doctor Stark. He put his stethoscope in his ears and listened to his patient's chest, stomach, back, and neck. He examined Ogden's eyes and ears. Then he stuck a thermometer in Ogden's mouth and watched the soap opera for three minutes, even though he couldn't hear what the actors were saying, since Ogden had to keep his mouth closed. Finally Doctor Stark took the thermometer out again.

"No fever," he said. "Ogden, I'm afraid there's nothing I can do for you."

"But he can't even speak for himself," Mr. Pettibone protested. "Is it something like laryngitis?"

"It's a much more difficult case than that, I'm afraid. Ogden has televisionosis."

"Televisionosis?" Ogden wanted to ask. Mr. Pettibone asked it for him.

"Yes," Doctor Stark replied. "It's a disease so rare it's practically unheard of. I've certainly never heard of it before. One of my patients used to get radio stations on his tooth fillings, but this is much more severe. Your boy is exhibiting all the symptoms of a television set."

"But he doesn't want to be a television set."

"I'm afraid he has no choice. There's no known cure for televisionosis."

"Oh, my," said Mr. Pettibone, too stunned to say anything else.

"Perhaps he'll outgrow it," said the doctor pleasantly. "And if he doesn't, he'll be very popular. Everybody loves television."

Otis Takes Aim

by Beverly Cleary
Illustrated by Louis Darling

Otis Spofford is in the mood for some excitement at school. So he's been throwing spitballs in class. "Otis Spofford," warns his teacher, Mrs. Gitler, "if you throw one more spitball, I'll do something that will make you wish you'd never thought of spitballs." Could Otis resist a challenge like that? No way. One juicy spitball later . . .

Mrs. Gitler said, "I want you to throw spitballs for me."

The class gasped. Throw spitballs! Whoever heard of a teacher asking someone to throw spitballs?

Even Otis was startled. He didn't know what to think, but he wasn't going to let anyone know he was taken off guard. "Sure," he said. "Any special place you want me to throw them?"

"Into the wastebasket," answered Mrs. Gitler. "I want you to sit on a chair and throw spitballs into the basket."

Otis grinned. The idea of sitting in front of the class to shoot spitballs into the wastebasket pleased him.

But Mrs. Gitler said, "Take your paper, the chair, and the basket to the back of the room."

Otis took his time about moving the chair and the wastebasket.

"Quickly, Otis," said the teacher.

"Spitball Spofford," whispered Stewy.

Otis settled himself on the chair and tore off a piece of paper. After chewing it, he threw it into the wastebasket with enough force to make a noise. He was pleased when the whole class turned around to look at him.

"All right, people. There is no need to watch Otis. We all know what he looks like," said Mrs. Gitler, as she took her pitch pipe out of her desk and the class got out its music books.

Otis chewed and threw. At first, the boys and girls peeked over their shoulders at him, but Mrs. Gitler started the singing lesson with a song about a barnyard. The class had so much fun imitating the sounds of different animals that they all lost interest in Otis.

"Moo-moo," went the first row, taking the part of cows. The second row, who took the part of chickens, made such funny cackles that the whole class laughed and Mrs. Gitler had to start the song again.

Otis chewed more and more slowly. His mouth was dry and he began to feel lonesome all by himself at the back of the room. He stopped making spitballs altogether and sat looking out of the window. It had been raining, and drops of sparkling water dripped from the trees. How good they looked!

"Go on with your spitballs, Otis," Mrs. Gitler re-

minded him at the end of the song. Then she started the class on *Row, Row, Row,* which was one of their favorites.

Otis tore off another piece of paper. He took his time rolling it, because he did not feel much like making a spitball. He put it in his mouth and chewed very, very slowly. He tried counting to ten between each chew. His mouth felt drier and drier, and he decided he hated the taste of paper.

"Row, row, row your boat," sang the class.

Otis sighed. He did not want to give up and admit to Mrs. Gitler that he had had enough of spitballs. Not in front of the whole class.

"Gently down the stream," sang the class.

Gently down the stream, thought Otis. Why did everything have to make him think of water? Doggedly he kept at his spitballs, but he worked as slowly as he could. He was wondering how he could make his spit last until school was out. He ran his tongue around his mouth. Then he stuck it out as far as he could to see if it were swelling up and turning black. He could barely see the tip, which was still pink. That was a good sign. Maybe he could hold out.

"Merrily, merrily, merrily," trilled the class.

Suddenly the fire-drill bell rang. He was saved! Otis leaped from his chair and was first in line at the door. If only he could get to a drinking fountain, he knew he could make his spit last until school was out.

"Quickly, children," said Mrs. Gitler. "Get in line. Don't push, George. Come along, Austine."

As soon as the class was lined up two by two, Mrs. Gitler opened the door and marched the boys and girls rapidly through the hall and down the stairs. She walked beside Otis, who looked longingly at the drinking fountain as they passed. With Mrs. Gitler beside him, there was no way he could get to it. The more he thought about that drinking fountain, the drier his mouth felt. If he could just turn the handle and let the cool water flow into his mouth for one instant!

Outdoors, the air was cool and damp. Otis opened his mouth and drew in gasps of cool air. He didn't care if he looked like a goldfish.

"Spitball Spofford," the boys and girls whispered to him as he opened his mouth toward the sky in case it should begin to rain again.

When everyone was out of the building, the bell rang again. "All right, class, about face," ordered Mrs. Gitler.

The class turned. This left Otis and his partner at the end of the line instead of the beginning. Now it would be easier to get to the drinking fountain. As soon as the class reached the top of the stairs, Otis bent over so Mrs. Gitler would not see him and darted behind the line of boys and girls to the fountain. He turned the handle, and just as the stream of water rose almost to his mouth, he felt a hand on his shoulder. It was the principal. "You know that no one is supposed to leave his line during a fire drill," said Mr. Howe, and steered Otis back to his place in line.

If that isn't my luck, thought Otis. Now my spit will never last.

As the class entered the room again, Otis was tempted to go back to his seat and hope Mrs. Gitler would forget the whole thing. But he knew that if he did Stewy or Linda or someone else would probably remind her. Anyway, he was not going to give in until he had to. He returned to his chair at the back of the room and tore off another piece of paper. Mrs. Gitler ignored him. Slowly he chewed the spitball and pitched it into the wastebasket. He tore off another piece of paper and looked at the clock. Another hour to chew and throw. A long, long hour. A minute clicked by and after a long time, another.

Otis put the paper in his mouth but he did not chew it. He just held it there a minute and took it out again. He never wanted to taste paper again. Mrs. Gitler had won. He only hoped she would not find it out.

The teacher looked up from her desk. "Well, Otis?" she asked.

Otis tried to lick his lips, but his mouth was too dry. "I guess . . . I guess . . . I've run out of spit," he said.

"Are you sure you're through throwing spitballs?" Mrs. Gitler wanted to know.

Otis did not want to answer the question, but he had to. "Yes," he said in a small voice.

"You may go out and get a drink before you return to your seat." Mrs. Gitler's eyes twinkled and she looked as if she wanted to laugh.

Otis managed a sheepish halfway grin as he went out of the room. Then he ran down the hall to the drinking fountain. How wonderful the jet of cold water looked! He drank in great gulps, stopped to gasp for breath, and gulped some more. Never had anything tasted so good. Otis drank for a long time before he wiped his mouth on his sleeve. He drank for such a long time that Mrs. Gitler came out into the hall to see what had happened to him.

"Was making me throw spitballs my comeuppance?" Otis wanted to know.

Mrs. Gitler laughed. "It would be for some boys, but I'm not sure about you." Then she shook her head. "Otis, if only you would work as hard on your spelling as you do on mischief!"

"Aw . . ." muttered Otis, because he couldn't think of anything else to say.

Back at his desk, Otis found the class was no longer interested in what he had done. As far as they were concerned, the excitement was over. He also discovered that although he was no longer thirsty, he still had a funny taste in his mouth from chewing so much paper. As he worked at his spelling, it began to bother him more and more. He wished he had something to eat that would take away the awful papery taste.

He fished through his pockets to see what he could find. Maybe he had an old stick of gum or something. In among his rabbit's foot, yo-yo, and rubber bands, Otis's fingers found the bud of garlic he had grabbed from the kitchen that morning. He untangled it and looked at it. He wondered what it would taste like. He smelled it and decided it smelled bad and good at the same time. Hold-

ing it under his desk, he pulled off a section and peeled off the pinkish outside skin. He popped it into his mouth, bit, and for a terrible instant was sorry. Tears came to his eyes, his nose tingled, and he blew the air out of his mouth.

Instantly everyone sitting near him turned to look at him. Ellen wrinkled her nose. Austine held hers.

"Wow!" whispered Stewy. "What's that awful smell?"

Wow is right, thought Otis, as he gulped and blew again. He bit into the garlic once more. The second bite was not quite so bad as the first. Almost, but not quite. Trying to look as if he ate raw garlic all the time, he chewed a couple of times and blew again.

"Otis Spofford," Ellen said in a fierce whisper, "you stop that!"

Otis grinned. This was just what he wanted. Things were back to normal. He took a deep breath and blew as hard as he could at Ellen.

Dribble!

by Judy Blume
Illustrated by Roy Doty

Peter Hatcher, age nine, won his pet turtle, Dribble, at a birthday party. Peter has a lock and chain on his bedroom door to protect Dribble from his three-year-old brother, Fudge. But it takes more than locks and chains to keep Fudge in line.

I will never forget Friday, May tenth. It's the most important day of my life. It didn't start out that way. It started out ordinary. I went to school. I ate my lunch. I had gym. And then I walked home from school with Jimmy Fargo. We planned to meet at our special rock in the park as soon as we changed our clothes.

In the elevator I told Henry I was glad summer was coming. Henry said he was too. When I got out at my floor I walked down the hall and opened the door to my apartment. I took off my jacket and hung it in the closet. I put my books on the hall table next to my mother's purse. I went straight to my room to change my clothes and check Dribble.

The first thing I noticed was my chain latch. It was unhooked. My bedroom door was open. And there was a chair smack in the middle of my doorway. I nearly tumbled over it. I ran to my dresser to check Dribble. He wasn't there! His bowl with the rocks and water was there—but Dribble was gone.

I got really scared. I thought, *Maybe he died while I was at school and I didn't know about it.* So I rushed into the kitchen and hollered, "Mom . . . where's Dribble?" My mother was baking something. My brother sat on the kitchen floor, banging pots and pans together. "Be quiet!" I yelled at Fudge. "I can't hear anything with all that noise."

"What did you say, Peter?" my mother asked me.

"I said I can't find Dribble. Where is he?"

"You mean he's not in his bowl?" my mother asked.

I shook my head.

"Oh dear!" my mother said. "I hope he's not crawling around somewhere. You know I don't like the way he smells. I'm going to have a look in the bedrooms. You check in here, Peter."

My mother hurried off. I looked at my brother. He was smiling. "Fudge, do you know where Dribble is?" I asked calmly.

Fudge kept smiling.

"Did you take him? Did you, Fudge?" I asked not so calmly.

Fudge giggled and covered his mouth with his hands.

I yelled. "Where is he? What did you do with my turtle?"

No answer from Fudge. He banged his pots and pans together again. I yanked the pots out of his hand. I tried to speak softly. "Now tell me where Dribble is. Just tell me where my turtle is. I won't be mad if you tell me. Come on, Fudge . . . please."

Fudge looked up at me. "In tummy," he said.

"What do you mean, in tummy?" I asked, narrowing my eyes.

"Dribble in tummy!" he repeated.

"What tummy?" I shouted at my brother.

"This one," Fudge said, rubbing his stomach. "Dribble in this tummy! Right here!"

I decided to go along with his game. "Okay. How did he get in there, Fudge?" I asked.

Fudge stood up. He jumped up and down and sang out, "I ATE HIM . . . ATE HIM . . . ATE HIM!" Then he ran out of the room.

My mother came back into the kitchen. "Well, I just can't find him anywhere," she said. "I looked in all the dresser drawers and the bathroom cabinets and the shower and the tub and . . ."

"Mom," I said, shaking my head. "How could you?"

"How could I what, Peter?" Mom asked.

"How could you let him do it?"

"Let who do what, Peter?" Mom asked.

"LET FUDGE EAT DRIBBLE!" I screamed.

My mother started to mix whatever she was baking. "Don't be silly, Peter," she said. "Dribble is a turtle."

"HE ATE DRIBBLE!" I insisted.

"Peter Warren Hatcher! STOP SAYING THAT!" Mom hollered.

"Well, ask him. Go ahead and ask him," I told her.

Fudge was standing in the kitchen doorway with a big grin on his face. My mother picked him up and patted his head. "Fudgie," she said to him, "tell Mommy where brother's turtle is."

"In tummy," Fudge said.

"What tummy?" Mom asked.

"MINE!" Fudge laughed.

My mother put Fudge down on the kitchen counter where he couldn't get away from her. "Oh, you're fooling Mommy . . . right?"

"No fool!" Fudge said.

My mother turned very pale. "You really ate your brother's turtle?"

Big smile from Fudge.

"YOU MEAN THAT YOU PUT HIM IN YOUR MOUTH AND CHEWED HIM UP . . . LIKE THIS?" Mom made believe she was chewing.

"No," Fudge said.

A smile of relief crossed my mother's face. "Of course you didn't. It's just a joke." She put Fudge down on the floor and gave me a *look.*

Fudge babbled. "No chew. No chew. Gulp . . . gulp

. . . all gone turtle. Down Fudge's tummy."

Me and my mother stared at Fudge.

"You didn't!" Mom said.

"Did so!" Fudge said.

"No!" Mom shouted.

"Yes!" Fudge shouted back.

"Yes?" Mom asked weakly, holding onto a chair with both hands.

"Yes!" Fudge beamed.

My mother moaned and picked up my brother. "Oh no! My angel! My precious little baby! OH . . . NO . . ."

My mother didn't stop to think about my turtle. She didn't even give Dribble a thought. She didn't even stop to wonder how my turtle liked being swallowed by my brother. She ran to the phone with Fudge tucked under one arm. I followed. Mom dialed the operator and cried, "Oh help! This is an emergency. My baby ate a turtle . . . STOP THAT LAUGHING," my mother told the operator. "Send an ambulance right away—25 West 68th Street."

Mom hung up. She didn't look too well. Tears were running down her face. She put Fudge down on the floor. I couldn't understand why she was so upset. Fudge seemed just fine.

"Help me, Peter," Mom begged. "Get me blankets."

I ran into my brother's room. I grabbed two blankets from Fudge's bed. He was following me around with that silly grin on his face. I felt like giving him a pinch. How could he stand there looking so happy when he had my turtle inside him?

I delivered the blankets to my mother. She wrapped Fudge up in them and ran to the front door. I followed and grabbed her purse from the hall table. I figured she'd be glad I thought of that.

Out in the hall I pressed the elevator buzzer. We had to wait a few minutes. Mom paced up and down in front of the elevator. Fudge was cradled in her arms. He sucked his fingers and made that slurping noise I like. But all I could think of was Dribble.

Finally, the elevator got to our floor. There were three people in it besides Henry. "This is an emergency," Mom wailed. "The ambulance is waiting downstairs. Please hurry!"

"Yes, Mrs. Hatcher. Of course," Henry said. "I'll run her down just as fast as I can. No other stops."

Someone poked me in the back. I turned around. It was Mrs. Rudder. "What's the matter?" she whispered.

"It's my brother," I whispered back. "He ate my turtle."

Mrs. Rudder whispered *that* to the man next to her and *he* whispered it to the lady next to *him* who whispered it to Henry. I faced front and pretended I didn't hear anything.

My mother turned around with Fudge in her arms and said, "That's not funny. Not funny at all!"

But Fudge said, "Funny, funny, funny Fudgie!"

Everybody laughed. Everybody except my mother.

The elevator door opened. Two men, dressed in white, were waiting with a stretcher. "This the baby?" one of them asked.

"Yes. Yes, it is," Mom sobbed.

"Don't worry, lady. We'll be to the hospital in no time."

"Come, Peter," my mother said, tugging at my sleeve. "We're going to ride in the ambulance with Fudge."

My mother and I climbed into the back of the blue ambulance. I was never in one before. It was neat. Fudge kneeled on a cot and peered out through the window. He waved at the crowd of people that had gathered on the sidewalk.

One of the attendants sat in back with us. The other one was driving. "What seems to be the trouble, lady?" the attendant asked. "This kid looks pretty healthy to me."

"He swallowed a turtle," my mother whispered.

"He did WHAT?" the attendant asked.

"Ate my turtle. That's what!" I told him.

My mother covered her face with her hanky and started to cry again.

"Hey, Joe!" the attendant called to the driver. "Make it snappy . . . *this* one swallowed a turtle!"

"That's not funny!" Mom insisted. I didn't think so either, considering it was my turtle!

We arrived at the back door of the hospital. Fudge was whisked away by two nurses. My mother ran after him. "You wait here, young man," another nurse called to me, pointing to a bench.

I sat down on the hard, wooden bench. I didn't have anything to do. There weren't any books or magazines spread out, like when I go to Dr. Cone's office. So I watched the clock and read all the signs on the walls. I found out I was in the emergency section of the hospital.

After a while the nurse came back. She gave me some paper and crayons. "Here you are. Be a good boy and draw some pictures. Your mother will be out soon."

I wondered if she knew about Dribble and that's why she was trying to be nice to me. I didn't feel like drawing any pictures. I wondered what they were doing to Fudge in there. Maybe he wasn't such a bad little guy after all. I remembered that Jimmy Fargo's little cousin once swallowed the most valuable rock from Jimmy's collection. And my mother told me that when I was a little kid I swallowed a quarter. Still . . . a quarter's not like a turtle!

I watched the clock on the wall for an hour and ten minutes. Then a door opened and my mother stepped out with Dr. Cone. I was surprised to see him. I didn't know he worked in the hospital.

"Hello, Peter," he said.

"Hello, Dr. Cone. Did you get my turtle?"

"Not yet, Peter," he said. "But I do have something to

show you. Here are some X-rays of your brother."

I studied the X-rays as Dr. Cone pointed things out to me.

"You see," he said. "There's your turtle . . . right there."

I looked hard. "Will Dribble be in there forever?" I asked.

"No. Definitely not! We'll get him out. We gave Fudge some medicine already. That should do the trick nicely."

"What kind of medicine?" I asked. "What trick?"

"Castor oil, Peter," my mother said. "Fudge took castor oil. And milk of magnesia. And prune juice too. Lots of that. All those things will help to get Dribble out of Fudge's tummy."

"We just have to wait," Dr. Cone said. "Probably until tomorrow or the day after. Fudge will have to spend the night here. But I don't think he's going to be swallowing anything that he isn't supposed to be swallowing from now on."

"How about Dribble?" I asked. "Will Dribble be all right?" My mother and Dr. Cone looked at each other. I knew the answer before he shook his head and said, "I think you may have to get a new turtle, Peter."

"I don't want a new turtle!" I said. Tears came to my eyes. I was embarrassed and wiped them away with the back of my hand. Then my nose started to run and I had to sniffle. "I want Dribble," I said. "That's the only turtle I want."

My mother took me home in a taxi. She told me my father was on his way to the hospital to be with Fudge. When we got home she made me lamb chops for dinner, but I wasn't very hungry. My father came home late that night. I was still up. My father looked gloomy. He whispered to my mother, "Not yet . . . nothing yet."

The next day was Saturday. No school. I spent the whole day in the hospital waiting room. There were plenty of people around. And magazines and books too. It wasn't like the hard bench in the emergency hallway. It was more like a living room. I told everybody that my brother ate my turtle. They looked at me kind of funny. But nobody ever said they were sorry to hear about my turtle. Never once.

My mother joined me for supper in the hospital coffee shop. I ordered a hamburger but I left most of it. Because right in the middle of supper my mother told me that if the medicine didn't work soon Fudge might have to have an operation to get Dribble out of him. My mother didn't eat anything.

That night my grandmother came to stay with me. My mother and father stayed at the hospital with Fudge. Things were pretty dreary at home. Every hour the phone rang. It was my mother calling from the hospital with a report.

"Not yet . . . I see," Grandma repeated. "Nothing happening yet."

I was miserable. I was lonely. Grandma didn't notice. I even missed Fudge banging his pots and pans together. In the middle of the night the phone rang again. It woke me up and I crept out into the hallway to hear what was going on.

Grandma shouted, "Whoopee! It's out! Good news at last."

She hung up and turned to me. "The medicine has finally worked, Peter. All that castor oil and milk of magnesia and prune juice finally worked. The turtle is out!"

"Alive or dead?" I asked.

"PETER WARREN HATCHER. WHAT A QUESTION!" Grandma shouted.

So my brother no longer had a turtle inside of him. And I no longer had a turtle! I didn't like Fudge as much as I thought I did before the phone rang.

The Tongue-twister

by B. Wiseman

Do you want to see how angry a moose can make a bear? Read this story about Morris and Boris, two surprisingly good friends.

"Can you say a tongue-twister?" Boris asked.

Morris said, "A tongue-twister."

"That is just the name of it," Boris said. "What you must say is: Peter Piper picked a peck of pickled peppers."

Morris asked, "What is a peck?"

Boris said, "A peck is a lot of something. Go on, say it."

Morris said, "A peck is a lot of something."

"No! No!" Boris cried. "Say the whole thing!"

Morris said, "The whole thing."

"No! No! NO!" Boris shouted. "Say: Peter Piper picked a peck of pickled peppers!"

Morris asked, "What are pickled peppers?"

Boris said, "Come with me . . . These are peppers. Pickled peppers are peppers you put in a pot and pickle. To pickle means to make sour. Now say the tongue-twister."

Morris said, "Peter Piper picked a peck of peppers and put them in a pot and pickled them."

"NO!" Boris cried. "Peter Piper picked a peck of pickled peppers!"

Morris asked, "How could Peter Piper pick a peck of pickled peppers? Pickled peppers are peppers you put in a pot and pickle!"

"I KNOW THAT!" Boris shouted. "But in the tongue-twister, Peter Pepper . . ."

Morris said, "You mean Peter Piper."

"YES!" Boris yelled. "Peter Piper! In the tongue-twister, Peter Piper pecked a pick . . ."

Morris cried, "You mean picked a peck!"

"YES! YES!" Boris roared. "Picked a peck! In the tongue-twister, Peter Piper picked a peck of pickled pots! No! I mean Peter Piper picked a pot of pickled pecks! No! No! Oh, you got me all mixed up! You will never learn to say a tongue-twister!"

And Boris went away.

A bird asked Morris, "Why was Boris yelling?"

Morris said, "Because I could not say: Peter Piper picked a peck of pickled peppers."

2

LET'S MAKE A DILL
SPECIAL
ALL
RIDDLES
DRASTICALLY
REDUCED!

Jokes and Riddles

Q: Who is beautiful, gray, and wears glass slippers?
A: Cinderelephant.

Q: What is gray, weighs two tons, and has wings?
A: Cinderelephant's fairy godmother.

JACK: What did the elephant rock 'n' roll star say into the microphone?
JILL: I don't know. What?
JACK: "Tusking—one, two, three. Tusking—one, two, three."

MACK: I can lift an elephant with one hand.
MOE: I don't believe you.
MACK: Get me an elephant with one hand and I'll show you.

SAL: What is the difference between an elephant and a mattababy?
SUE: What's a mattababy?
SAL: Why, nothing. What's the matter with you?

BOB: Why do elephants paint their toenails red?
BETTY: I don't know. Why?
BOB: So they can hide in the strawberry patch.
BETTY: I don't believe that.
BOB: Did you ever see an elephant in a strawberry patch?
BETTY: No!
BOB: See? It works!

Q: When is an elephant like a cute little bunny rabbit?
A: When he's wearing his cute little bunny rabbit suit.

TEACHER: Frankie, can you define "nonsense"?
FRANKIE: An elephant hanging over a cliff with his tail wrapped around a daisy.

Q: What time is it when a elephant sits on a park bench?
A: Time to get a new bench.

Q: What do you get if you cross an elephant with a canary?
A: A pretty messy cage.

Q: What do you find between elephants' toes?
A: Slow-running people.

Q: How do you stop an elephant from charging?
A: Take away his credit cards.

Q: How do you make an elephant float?
A: Put two scoops of ice cream, some milk, and soda water in a glass. Add one elephant.

Q: How do you get five elephants into a Volkswagen?
A: Put two in front, two in back, and one in the glove compartment.

Q: How can you tell when there's an elephant in the back seat of your car?
A: You can smell the peanuts on its breath.

Q: Who started all these elephant jokes?
A: That's what the elephants want to know.

Q: What do you call a hamburger bun in a rocking chair?
A: Rockin' roll.

Q: What TV show do pickles like best?
A: "Let's Make a Dill."

Q: What's green, noisy, and very dangerous?
A: A herd of stampeding pickles.

Q: What do cowboys put on their pancakes?
A: Maple stirrup.

Q: What do you call a banana that has been stepped on?
A: A banana splat.

Q: What's the best thing to put into a pie?
A: Your teeth.

DINER: Is there any soup on the menu?
WAITER: There was, but I wiped it off.

Q: What do you get when you cross a chicken with a dog?
A: Pooched eggs.

Q: What do you call a fish with two knees?
A: A two-knee fish.

Q: What did the mayonnaise say to the refrigerator?
A: "Close the door. I'm dressing."

The restaurant sign said, "We Fought the Roaches," so the man went in and ordered soup.
MAN: Waiter, why is there a roach in my soup? The sign said you fought the roaches.
WAITER: It didn't say we won.

Q: What do you get when you cross a frog and a potato?
A: A potatoad.

Q: What does a shark eat with peanut butter?
A: Jellyfish.

Q: Name five things that contain milk.
A: Butter, cheese, ice cream, and two cows.

WAITER: Shall I cut your pizza into six or twelve pieces?
CUSTOMER: Only six, please. I couldn't possibly eat twelve pieces.

WAITER: Have you tried the meatballs, sir?
CUSTOMER: Yes—and I found them guilty.

CUSTOMER: What is this fly doing in my soup?
WAITER: Looks like the backstroke to me.

CUSTOMER: Waiter, there's a fly drowning in my soup!
WAITER: Quick, give him mouth-to-mouth resuscitation!

CUSTOMER: Waiter, there's a fly in my black bean soup!
WAITER: Very well, madam. I'll take it to the chef and he'll exchange it for a bean.

CUSTOMER: Waiter, there's a fly in my soup.
WAITER: Don't worry about it. He won't eat too much.

CUSTOMER: Waiter, there's a dead fly in my soup!
WAITER: It's the heat that kills them, sir.

CUSTOMER: What is this fly doing in my ice cream?
WAITER: He must like winter sports.

TEACHER: If you stood with your back to the north and faced due south, what would be on your left hand?
DEBBIE: Fingers.

TEACHER: If you add 500, 391, 38, 162, and 17, then divide by 39, what would you get?
STUART: The wrong answer.

TEACHER: Oscar, if you had five pieces of candy and Joey asked you for one, how many pieces would you have left?
OSCAR: Five.

TEACHER: How did you get that horrible swelling on your nose?
SMART SCOTT: I bent over to smell a brose.
TEACHER: There's no *b* in rose.
SMART SCOTT: There was in this one.

TEACHER: Yes, what is it?

FAILING STUDENT: I don't want to frighten you, but Dad said that if I don't get better grades, someone's going to get a spanking.

TEACHER: Suzie, please spell "cattle."

SUZIE: C-A-T-T-T-L-E.

TEACHER: Leave out one of the *t*'s.

SUZIE: Which one?

TEACHER: It's the law of gravity that keeps us from falling off the earth.

SILLY SALLY: What kept us from falling off before the law was passed?

ARNIE: I wish I had been born a thousand years ago.

LES: Why?

ARNIE: Just think of all the history I wouldn't have to study.

TEACHER: Donald, I hope I didn't see you looking at Annie's paper.

DONALD: I hope you didn't either!

TEACHER: Birds, though small, are remarkable creatures. For example, what can a bird do that I can't do?

EAGER EARL: Take a bath in a saucer.

TEACHER: Name the four seasons.
STUDENT: Salt, pepper, sugar, and spice.

STUDENT: I don't think I deserve a zero on this test.
TEACHER: Neither do I. But it's the lowest grade I can give you.

FATHER: Why is your January report card marked so low?
SON: Well, you know how it is, Dad. After Christmas everything is marked down.

"Say, Mom," said Steve. "There's a special PTA meeting at school this afternoon."
"Really?" said his mother. "What's so special about it?"
"It's just for you," said Steve. "Oh yes, the principal, my teacher, and I have been invited, too."

The boy came home from school with a zero on his paper.
"Why did you get the zero?" his mother asked.
"That's no zero," the boy answered.
"Teacher ran out of stars, so she gave me the moon."

MATH TEACHER: And so we find that X equals zero.
STUDENT: Gee. All that work for nothing.

TEACHER: You can't sleep in my class!
STUDENT: I could if you didn't talk so loudly.

TEACHER: Frank, if you found three dollars in your right pocket and two dollars in your left pocket, what would you have?
FRANK: Somebody else's pants on.

JACK: Hooray! The teacher said we would have a test—rain or shine.
JOAN: But that's nothing to be happy about.
JACK: It's snowing.

TEACHER: If I lay one egg on this chair and two on the table, how many will I have altogether?
SYLVESTER: Personally, I don't believe you can do it.

DAUGHTER: Dad, can you write your name in the dark?
DAD: I think so.
DAUGHTER: Great. Would you please turn off the lights and sign my report card?

A boy wrote this letter from boarding school:
Dear Mom and Dad:
Gue$$ what I need? Plea$e $end $ome $oon.
Be$t Wi$he$,
Your $on, $ammy
The parents' reply:
Dear Sammy:
NOthing much is happening here. Please write aNOther letter soon. Bye for NOw.
Love,
Dad and Mom

VOICE ON THE PHONE: Is this the principal?
PRINCIPAL: Yes.
VOICE ON THE PHONE: Jenny Smith is too sick to come to school today.
PRINCIPAL: Who's calling, please?
VOICE ON THE PHONE: This is my mother.

Q: Where do sheep get their hair cut?
A: At the baa-baa shop.

Q: Why did they fire the goose from the basketball team?
A: Too many fowl plays.

Q: Who saw the Brontosaurus enter the restaurant?
A: The diners saw.

Q: What happened to the cat who swallowed a flashlight?
A: He hiccuped with delight.

Q: Why is it hard to talk with a goat around?
A: Because he keeps butting in.

Q: On the way to the water hole, a zebra met four elephants. Each elephant had three monkeys on its back. Each monkey had two birds on its tail. How many animals in all were going to the water hole?
A: Only one. The rest were coming back from the water hole.

Q: What dog says "meow"?
A: A police dog working undercover.

Q: What kind of key won't open a door?
A: A monkey.

Q: Why does a mother kangaroo hope it doesn't rain?
A: She hates it when the children have to stay inside.

Q: What do you call a sleeping bull?
A: A bulldozer.

ANN: Did you hear about the cat who swallowed a ball of yarn?
AL: No, tell me.
ANN: She had mittens.

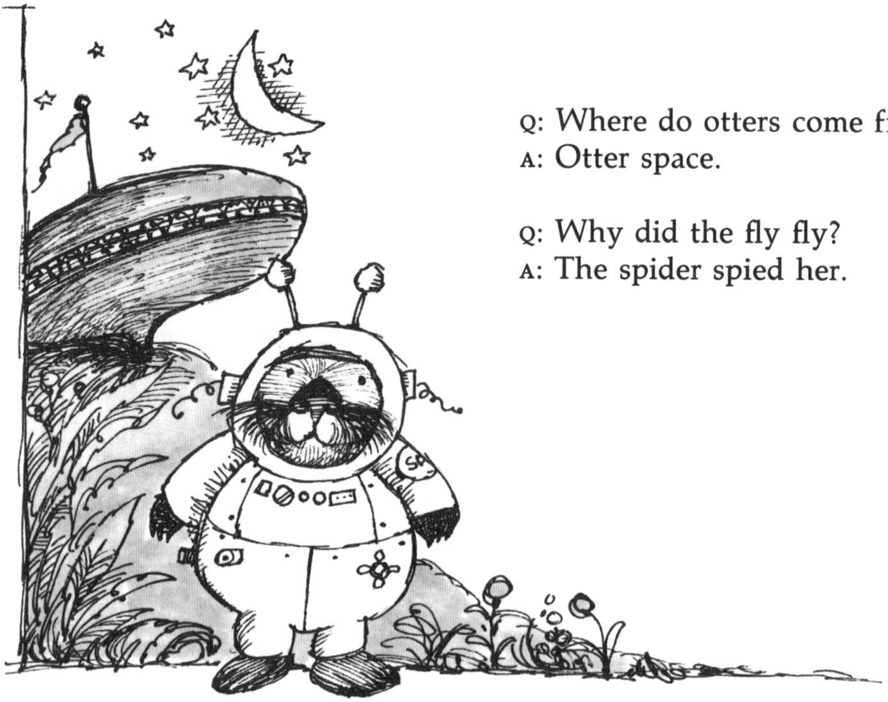

Q: Where do otters come from?
A: Otter space.

Q: Why did the fly fly?
A: The spider spied her.

Q: Why did they let a turkey join the band?
A: He had the drumsticks.

Q: Why do cows wear bells?
A: Their horns don't work.

Q: Why did the chicken cross the road?
A: The light was green.

Q: Why did the chicken want to get to the other side?
A: It wanted to see a man lay bricks.

Q: Why did the duck cross the road?
A: The chicken was on vacation.

ANN: My dog is a baseball dog.
STAN: What makes him a baseball dog?
ANN: He catches flies, chases fowls, and beats it for home when he sees the catcher coming.

Q: Why don't ducks tell jokes while they are flying?
A: Because they would quack up.

Q: Why do bees hum?
A: They don't know the words.

Q: What happens to a cat who eats a lemon?
A: It turns into a sourpuss.

Q: Why did Snoopy quit?
A: He was tired of working for Peanuts.

Q: Who performs operations at the fish hospital?
A: The head sturgeon.

Q: What is smarter than a talking horse?
A: A spelling bee.

Q: What do you call a rabbit with fleas?
A: Bugs Bunny.

Q: What do you call two spiders who just got married?
A: Newlywebs.

Q: What is green, has six legs, and can jump over your head?
A: A grasshopper with the hiccups.

Q: Where do cows go on dates?
A: To the moo-vies.

LITTLE WORM: Am I late, Mother?
MOTHER WORM: Yes, where in earth have you been?

BOY: I'd like a quarter's worth of birdseed, please.
STOREKEEPER: How many birds do you have?
BOY: None, but I want to grow some.

Q: What goes 999-*thump,* 999-*thump,* 999-*thump?*
A: A centipede with a wooden leg.

Q: What has four legs and goes "Oom! Oom!"?
A: A cow walking backward.

Q: What's the best way to catch a rabbit?
A: Hide behind a bush and make a noise like a carrot.

Q: What has four legs and flies?
A: A horse in the summertime.

Q: How does a hippopotamus get up a tree?
A: Climbs on an acorn and waits.

Q: How does a hippopotamus get down from a tree?
A: He sits on a leaf and waits for the fall.

Knock, knock.
Who's there?
Pencil.
Pencil who?
Pencil fall down if
you don't wear a belt.

Knock, knock.
Who's there?
Tuscaloosa.
Tuscaloosa who?
Tuscaloosa on
older elephants.

Knock, knock.
Who's there?
Boo.
Boo who?
Don't cry.
It's only a joke!

Knock, knock.
Who's there?
Diesel.
Diesel who?
Diesel make you laugh
if you're not too smart.

Knock, knock.
Who's there?
Turnip.
Turnip who?
Turnip your pants—
they're too long.

Knock, knock.
  Who's there?
Banana.
  Banana who?
Knock, knock.
  Who's there?
Banana.
  Banana who?
Knock, knock.
  Who's there?
Orange.
  Orange who?
Orange you glad I didn't say banana?

Knock, knock.
Who's there?
Mandy.
Mandy who?
Mandy lifeboats!

Knock, knock.
Who's there?
Tuba.
Tuba who?
Tuba toothpaste.

Knock, knock.
Who's there?
Fire engine.
Fire engine who?
Fire engine one and prepare for blast-off!

Knock, knock.
Who's there?
Lettuce.
Lettuce who?
Lettuce in. It's cold out here.

Knock, knock.
Who's there?
Philip.
Philip who?
Philip the tub. I want to take a bath.

Knock, knock.
Who's there?
Tim.
Tim who?
Tim-ber!!

Knock, knock.
Who's there?
Little old lady.
Little old lady who?
I didn't know
you could yodel.

Knock, knock.
Who's there?
Wooden.
Wooden who?
Wooden you
like to know.

Knock, knock.
Who's there?
Hammond.
Hammond who?
Hammond eggs
is good for breakfast.

Knock, knock.
Who's there?
Farm.
Farm who?
Farm-e to know and
you to find out.

Knock, knock.
Who's there?
Hoo.
Hoo who?
What are you, an owl?

Knock, knock.
Who's there?
Russell.
Russell who?
Russell me up
something to eat.

Knock, knock.
Who's there?
Dishes.
Dishes who?
Dishes your mother!
Now open the door!

Knock, knock.
Who's there?
Hatch.
Hatch who?
Gesundheit!

Knock, knock.
Who's there?
Police.
Police who?
Police open up.
I forgot
my lunch.

Knock, knock.
Who's there?
Roach.
Roach who?
Roach you a letter, but you didn't answer.
Knock, knock.
Who's there?
I am.
I am who?
You mean you don't know?
Knock, knock.
Who's there?
Sir.
Sir who?
Sir-prise!
Knock, knock.
Who's there?
Tinker Bell.
Tinker Bell who?
Tinker Bell is out of order.
IT MUST BE HALLOWEEN.

DOCTOR: What's the matter with your wife?
HUSBAND: She thinks she's a chicken.
DOCTOR: That's terrible. How long has she been this way?
HUSBAND: For three years.
DOCTOR: Why didn't you bring her to see me sooner?
HUSBAND: We needed the eggs.

PATIENT: My foot falls asleep and wakes me up.
DOCTOR: If your foot is asleep, how can it wake you up?
PATIENT: It snores.

LOU: I think I'm sick. Call me a doctor.
SUE: Okay. You're a doctor.

PATIENT: My stomach's been aching ever since I ate those twelve oysters yesterday.
DOCTOR: Were they fresh?
PATIENT: I don't know.
DOCTOR: Well, how did they look when you opened the shells?
PATIENT: You're supposed to open the shells?

PATIENT: I was just bitten on the leg by a dog.
DOCTOR: Did you put anything on it?
PATIENT: No. He liked it just the way it was.

BOY: Did you hear about the new doctor doll?
GIRL: No. What's it like?
BOY: You wind it up and it operates on batteries.

PATIENT: Doctor, you must help me. I can't remember anything.
DOCTOR: How long has this been going on?
PATIENT: How long has *what* been going on?

PATIENT: I am not well, Doctor.
DOCTOR: What seems to be the trouble?
PATIENT: I work like a horse, eat like a bird, and I'm as tired as a dog.
DOCTOR: Sounds to me like you ought to see a veterinarian.

PATIENT: Doctor, you have to help me. I snore so loud I wake myself up.
DOCTOR: Then you'll have to sleep in another room.

PATIENT: Doctor, I think corn is growing out of my ears.
DOCTOR: Why, so it is. How did this happen?
PATIENT: Beats me. I planted radishes.

PATIENT: Oh! Ouch! Oh! Ouch!
DOCTOR: Stop yelling. I haven't put the needle in yet.
PATIENT: I know. But you're standing on my foot.

PATIENT: Doctor, that ointment you gave me makes my arm smart.
DOCTOR: In that case, rub some on your head.

DOCTOR: I'm afraid you have canary disease.
PATIENT: Can you cure me, Doc?
DOCTOR: Yes, it's tweetable.

PATIENT: I just swallowed my harmonica. What should I do?
DOCTOR: Be happy.
PATIENT: Be happy about what?
DOCTOR: Be happy you weren't playing the piano.

DOCTOR: Stick out your tongue.
PATIENT: What for? I'm not mad at you.

PATIENT: Doctor, last night I dreamed I ate a giant marshmallow.
DOCTOR: What's so bad about that?
PATIENT: When I woke up, the pillow was gone.

MRS. JONES: Doctor, my husband thinks he's a parking meter.

PSYCHIATRIST: That's serious. Have him come to see me this Friday.

MRS. JONES: I'm sorry, he can't make it. Friday is the day they come and take the coins out of his mouth.

PSYCHIATRIST: Mr. Johnson, I think you're suffering from a split personality.
MR. JOHNSON: No, we aren't.

PATIENT: Doctor, I have this terrible problem when I go shopping. I take home everything that's marked down.
PSYCHIATRIST: Why is that such a problem?
PATIENT: Last week I took home an escalator.

PSYCHIATRIST: What do you dream about at night?
PATIENT: Baseball.
DOCTOR: Don't you dream about anything else?
PATIENT: What—and miss my turn at bat?

"There's nothing wrong with you," said the psychiatrist to his patient. "Why, you're as sane as I am."

"But, Doctor!" said the patient as he brushed wildly at himself. "It's the butterflies! They're all over me!"

"For heaven's sake," cried the doctor. "Don't brush them off on me!"

Psychiatrists tell us that one out of four people is mentally ill. So check your friends—if three of them seem to be all right, you're the one.

Dentist Jokes

DENTIST: Good grief. You have the biggest cavity I've ever seen . . . ever seen . . . ever seen.

PATIENT: You don't have to repeat yourself.

DENTIST: I didn't. That was an echo.

Veterinarian Jokes

DOG OWNER: I'm worried, Doc. I think my dog has ticks. What should I do?

VETERINARIAN: Don't wind him.

Q: What do you call an operation on a rabbit?

A: A hare-cut.

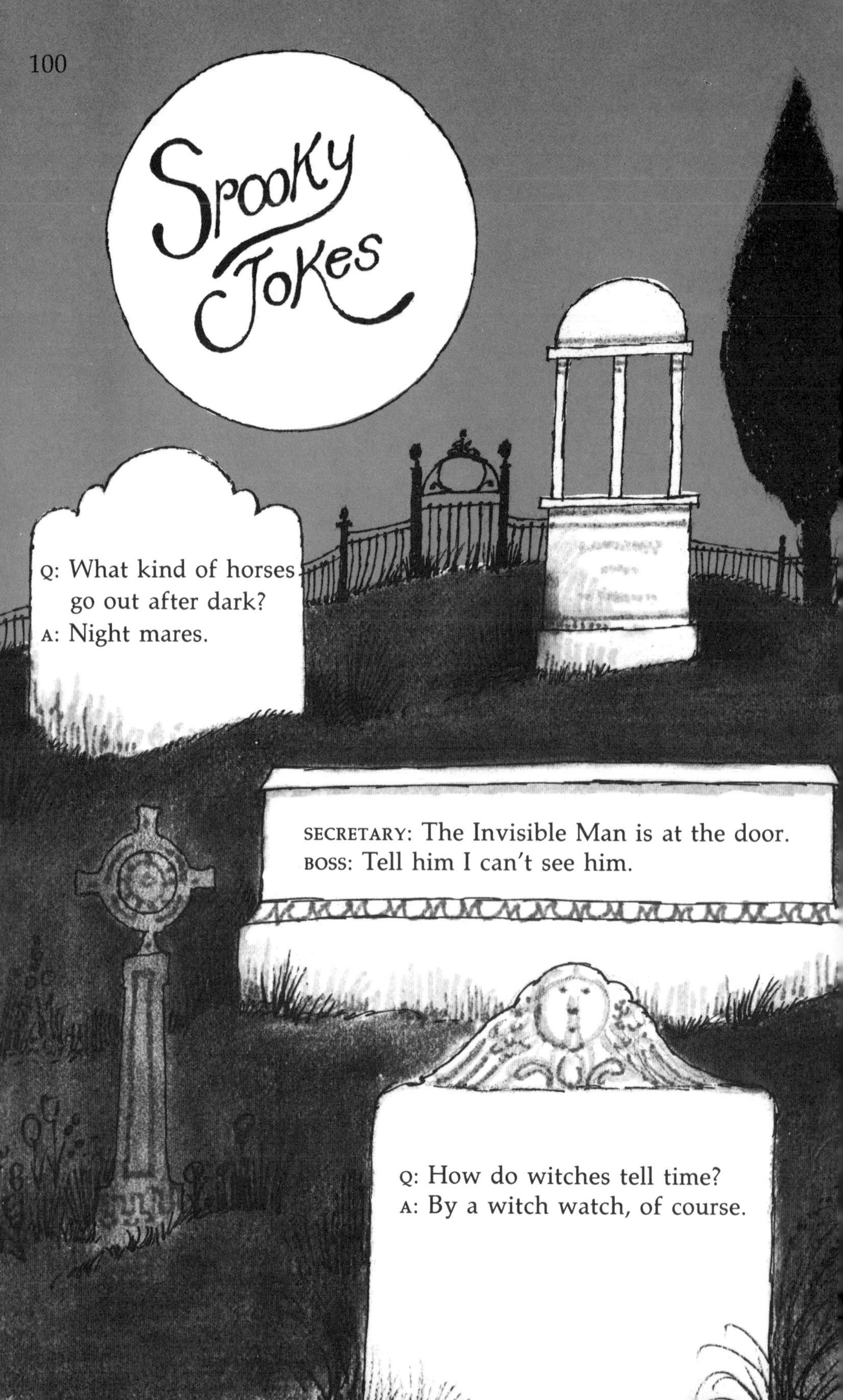

Spooky Jokes

Q: What kind of horses go out after dark?
A: Night mares.

SECRETARY: The Invisible Man is at the door.
BOSS: Tell him I can't see him.

Q: How do witches tell time?
A: By a witch watch, of course.

Q: What did the father ghost tell the little ghost?
A: "Don't spook until you're spooken to."
Q: What do you get when you cross peanut butter, bread, jelly, and a werewolf?
A: A peanut butter and jelly sandwich that howls and gets hairy when the full moon rises.

Q: Why was the witch first in her class?
A: She was the best speller.

Q: What was the first place Dracula visited when he went to New York?
A: The Vampire State Building.
Q: Why didn't they want him hanging around?
A: Because he was a pain in the neck.

CHILD: Mommy, all the kids say I look like a werewolf.
MOTHER: Shut up and comb your face.

Q: Why does the Frankenstein monster look so stiff when he walks?
A: Because Mrs. Frankenstein put too much starch in his underwear.

Q: What do sea monsters eat?
A: Fish and ships.

Q: What is a ghost's favorite food?
A: Spook-ghetti.

Q: How do you greet a three-headed monster?
A: "Hello. Hello. Hello. How are you? How are you? How are you?"

Q: What is a monster's normal eyesight?
A: 20-20-20-20-20.

Q: What was the vampire doing on the highway?
A: Looking for the main artery.

MONSTER ONE: That girl over there rolled her eyes at me. What should I do?
MONSTER TWO: If you are a real gentleman, you will pick them up and roll them back to her.

MONSTER ONE: Did you hear about Freddy? He died when he drank a gallon of varnish.
MONSTER TWO: That's too bad.
MONSTER ONE: Yes, but they say he had a lovely finish.

Q: What did the witch's broom say to her baby?
A: "Go to sweep, little baby."

Q: What do you call a skeleton that pushes your doorbell?
A: A dead ringer.

BABY: Mommy, what's a vampire?
MOTHER: Don't ask silly questions. Drink your tomato juice before it clots.

Q: What do you get if you cross a monster with a parrot?
A: I don't know, but you give it a cracker when it asks for one.

The vampire took an ocean cruise. He went into the dining room and said, "I'm starving."

"Would you like to see a menu?" asked the waiter.

"No, just show me the passenger list," answered the vampire.

Q: What do you call a skeleton that won't get out of bed?
A: Lazy bones.

Q: What do witches eat for dinner?
A: Halloweenies.

FIRST ASTRONAUT: What has 6 eyes, 10 arms, and is green all over?
SECOND ASTRONAUT: I don't know.
FIRST ASTRONAUT: I don't know either, but it's looking in our window.

TIM: Why do monsters have square shoulders?
JIM: Because they eat lots of cereal.
TIM: How can cereal give them square shoulders?
JIM: It's not the cereal. It's the boxes!

MONSTER MOTHER TO CHILD: I told you never to speak with someone in your mouth!

Q: Do vampires have holidays?
A: Sure. Haven't you ever heard of Fangsgiving Day?

FIRST MONSTER *(after catching an airplane in flight):* How do you eat one of these things?
SECOND MONSTER: Like a peanut. Just break it open and eat what's inside!

CHILD MONSTER: Mother, I hate my teacher.
MOTHER MONSTER: Then just eat your salad.

Q: Why didn't the skeleton have a good time at the prom?
A: He had no body to dance with.

Dr. Frankenstein sent Igor to get two fresh bodies. Igor went to the cemetery and dug up two bodies from a grave marked "John and Grace Hill." While Dr. Frankenstein worked on the bodies, he asked Igor to play some music on the radio. As soon as the music started, the two bodies came to life and got up from the table.

Igor said, "The Hills are alive with the sound of music."

Dracula was lying in his coffin sleeping one bright, sunny day. For a prank, some boys nailed roller skates to the coffin and sent it rolling down a hill. It narrowly missed people and cars and went crashing through a drugstore window. As the coffin sped through the drugstore, the startled pharmacist heard Dracula say, "You got anything to help stop this coffin?"

"I love hot dogs," Tom said frankly.

"These jeans are too tight," Tom panted.

"Let's go to the rodeo," Tom said hoarsely.

"I'm raising a billy goat," Tom said gruffly.

"Can't you keep that dog quiet?" Tom barked.

"I brought you these candies," Tom said sweetly.

"I hear an owl," Tom hooted.

"Is this sweater 100 percent wool?" asked Tom sheepishly.

Q: Why doesn't a bike stand up by itself?
A: It's two-tired.

Q: Why is 6 afraid of 7?
A: Because 7 8 9!

Q: What did the rug say to the floor?
A: "Stay where you are. I've got you covered."

Q: What did the judge say when a skunk walked into the court room?
A: "Odor in the court!"

Q: Can a person have a nose twelve inches long?
A: No. Then it would be a foot.

GIRL: Where does the Lone Ranger take his garbage?
BOY: To the dump, to the dump, to the dump, dump, dump.

JAKE: Where did King Richard III keep his armies?
JACK: Up his sleevies.

Q: What's purple and conquered the world?
A: Alexander the Grape.

Q: What's the happiest state in the Union?
A: Merry-land. (Maryland.)

Q: How do you send a message in the forest?
A: By moss code.

Q: What's white and flies up?
A: A confused snowflake.

DAN: What's purple and green with yellow and black stripes and has a hundred legs?
DONNA: I don't know.
DAN: I don't know either, but it's crawling up your neck.

Q: What did one tonsil say to the other?
A: "Get dressed. The doctor's taking us out tonight."

Q: What did one flea say to the other when they came out of the theater?
A: "Shall we walk or take a dog?"

Q: What's white and black with a cherry on top?
A: A police car.

Q: What did the robot say to the gas pump?
A: "Take your finger out of your ear."

Q: How long is the song "Soap, Soap, Soap, Soap, Soap"?
A: About five bars.

Q: Why did the traffic light turn red?
A: So would you if you had to change in the middle of the street.

Q: Why did Humpty Dumpty have a great fall?
A: He wanted to make up for a bad summer.

Q: Why did the burglar take a bath?
A: He wanted to make a clean getaway.

Q: What did Cinderella say to the photographer?
A: "Someday my prints will come."

Q: Did you hear about the robbery at the laundromat?
A: Two clothespins held up a shirt.

Q: What did the beach say as the tide came in?
A: "Long time, no sea."

Q: What is the biggest jewel in the world?
A: A baseball diamond.

Q: What has hands but never washes its face?
A: A clock.

Q: What did one elevator say to the other?
A: "I think I'm coming down with something."

Q: What did one potato chip say to the other?
A: "Let's go for a dip."

3
ROW, ROW, ROW
YOUR GOAT
Funny Poems

Young Lady, Whose Nose

There is a young lady, whose nose,
Continually prospers and grows;
When it grew out of sight,
She exclaimed in a fright,
"Oh! Farewell to the end of my nose!"

Edward Lear

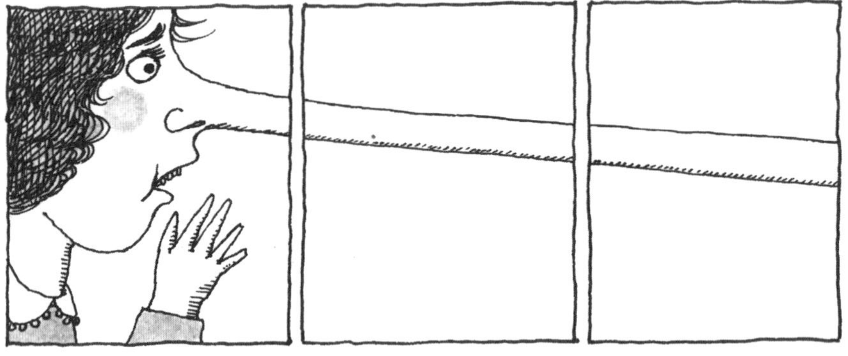

Young Lady of Spain

There was a young lady of Spain
Who was dreadfully sick on a train,
Not once, but again
And again and again,
And again and again and again.

Author Unknown

Old Man from Peru

There was an old man from Peru
Who dreamed he was eating his shoe.
In the midst of the night
He awoke in a fright
And found it was perfectly true!

Author Unknown

Old Man with a Beard

There was an Old Man with a beard
Who said, "It is just as I feared!
Two Owls and a Hen
Four Larks and a Wren
Have all built their nests in my beard!"

Edward Lear

Double Meanings

Wild Flowers

"Of what are you afraid, my child?" inquired
the kindly teacher.
"Oh, sir! the flowers, they are wild,"
replied the timid creature.

Peter Newell

Puzzling

Here's a fact that will cause you to frown—
Instead of growing up, a goose grows down!

William Cole

Night, Knight

"Night, night,"
said one knight
to the other knight
the other night.
"Night, night, knight."

Author Unknown

Rhododendron, of Course

A major, with wonderful force,
Called out in Hyde Park for a horse.
All the flowers looked round,
But no horse could be found,
So he just rhododendron, of course.

Author Unknown

Two Elephants

Two elephants went to the pool one day,
But the lifeguard there made them go away.
He said their swimsuits would never do,
For they only had one pair of trunks for two.

Madeleine Edmondson

Goops and Other Folks

The Goops

The Goops they lick their fingers,
  And the Goops they lick their knives;
They spill their broth on the tablecloth—
  Oh, they lead disgusting lives!
The Goops they talk while eating,
  And loud and fast they chew;
And that is why I'm glad that I
  Am not a Goop—are you?

Gelett Burgess

Speak Roughly to Your Little Boy

Speak roughly to your little boy,
  And beat him when he sneezes:
He only does it to annoy,
  Because he knows it teases.

Lewis Carroll

A Dirty Old Man

"Who are you?"
"A dirty old man;
I've always been so
Since the day I began.
Father and Mother
Were dirty before me,
Hot or cold water
Has never come o'er me."

English Nursery Rhyme

My Face

As a beauty I am not a star,
There are others more handsome,
    by far,
  But my face—I don't mind it
  For I am behind it.
It's the people in front get the jar!

Anthony Euwer

Through the Teeth

Through the teeth
And past the gums.
Look out, stomach,
Here it comes!

Traditional

Oyster Stew

An oyster met an oyster
  And they were oysters two;
Two oysters met two oysters
  And they were oysters too;
Four oysters met a pint of milk,
  And they were oyster stew!

Gyles Brandreth

The Catsup Bottle

Shake and shake
the catsup bottle.
None will come
and then a lot'll.

Richard Armour

Hot Dog

My father owns the butcher shop.
My mother cuts the meat.
And I'm the little hot dog
That runs around the street.

Traditional

Celery

Celery, raw,
Develops the jaw.
But celery, stewed,
Is more quietly chewed.

Ogden Nash

Never Take a Pig to Lunch

Never take a pig to lunch
Don't invite him home for brunch
Cancel chances to be fed
Till you're certain he's well-bred.

Quiz him! Can he use a spoon?
Does his sipping sing a tune?
Will he slurp and burp and snuff
Till his gurgling makes you gruff?

Would he wrap a napkin 'round
Where the dribbled gravy's found?
Tidbits nibble? Doughtnuts dunk?
Spill his milk before it's drunk?

Root and snoot through soup du jour?
Can your appetite endure?
If his manners make you moan
Better let him lunch alone.

Susan Alton Schmeltz

Boa Constrictor

Oh I'm being eaten by a boa constrictor,
A boa constrictor, a boa constrictor,
I'm being eaten by a boa constrictor,
And I don't like it . . . one bit!
Well what do you know . . . it's nibbling my toe,
Oh gee . . . it's up to my knee,
Oh my . . . it's up to my thigh,
Oh fiddle . . . it's up to my middle,
Oh heck . . . it's up to my neck,
Oh dread . . . it's . . . MMFFF.

Shel Silverstein
from *Where the Sidewalk Ends*

The Frog

What a wonderful bird the frog are—
When he stand, he sit almost
When he hop, he fly almost
He ain't got no sense hardly
He ain't got no tail hardly either
When he sit, he sit on what he ain't got almost!

Author Unknown

More Animals

Hippopotamus

See the handsome hippopotamus,
Wading on the river-bottomus.
He goes everywhere he wishes
In pursuit of little fishes.
Cooks them in his cooking-potamus.
"My," fish say, "he eats a lot-of-us!"

Joanna Cole

Perils of Thinking

A centipede was happy quite,
   Until a frog in fun
Said, "Pray, which leg comes after which?"
This raised her mind to such a pitch,
She lay distracted in the ditch
   Considering how to run.

Author Unknown

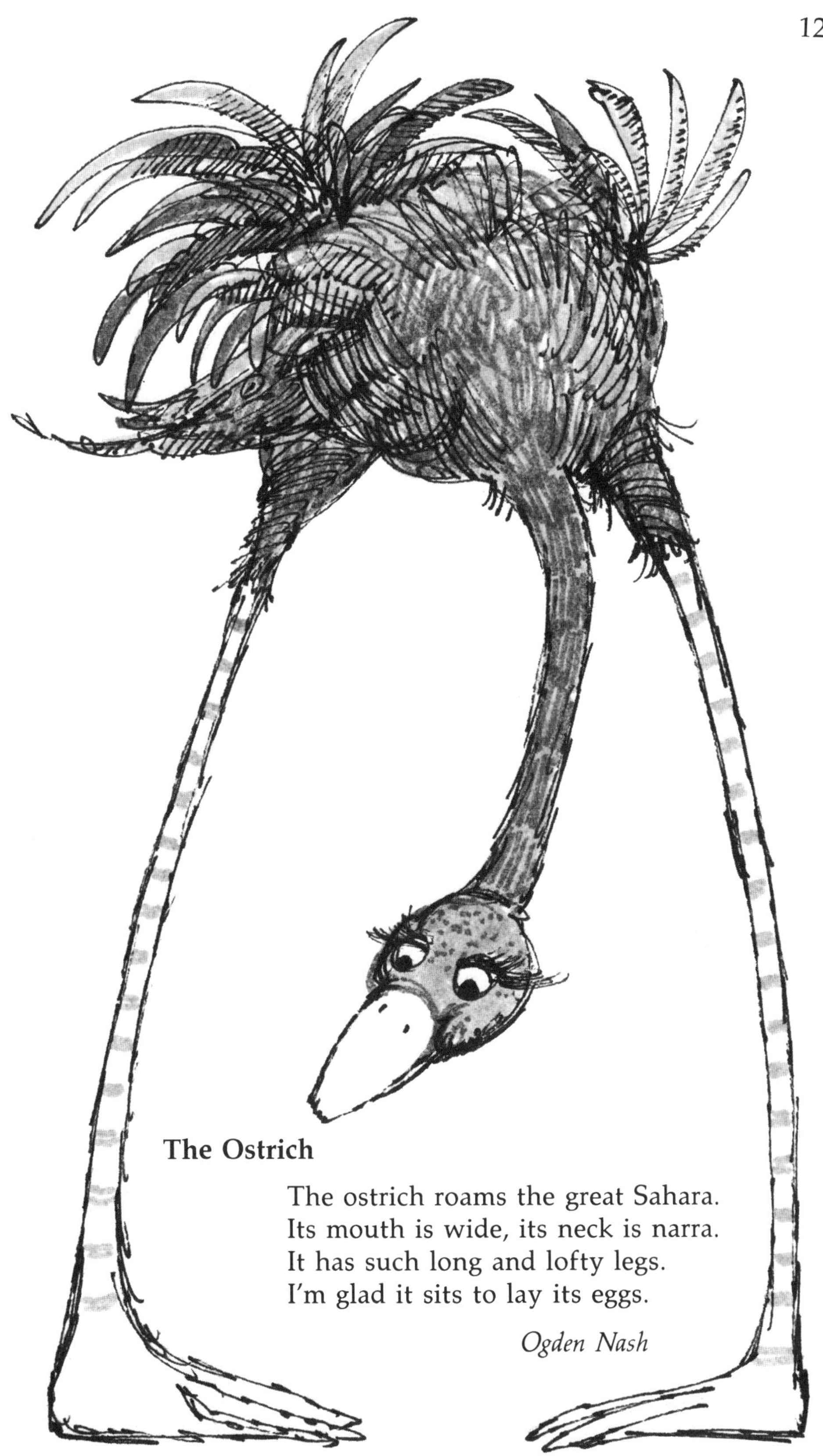

The Ostrich

The ostrich roams the great Sahara.
Its mouth is wide, its neck is narra.
It has such long and lofty legs.
I'm glad it sits to lay its eggs.

Ogden Nash

Eight Teasing Rhymes . . .

Marguerite, go wash your feet.
The Board of Health's across the street.

I saw you in the ocean.
I saw you in the sea.
I saw you in the bathtub.
Oops, pardon me!

Here comes the bride
Big, fat, and wide.
Here comes the groom
Stiff as a broom.

I see London,
I see France,
I see someone's
Underpants.

Cry, baby, cry,
Stick your finger in your eye
And tell your mother
It wasn't I.

Liar, liar
Your pants are on fire.
Your nose is as long
As a telephone wire.

Two's a couple
Three's a crowd
Four on the sidewalk's
Not allowed.

Melissa is so small
A rat could eat her, hat and all.

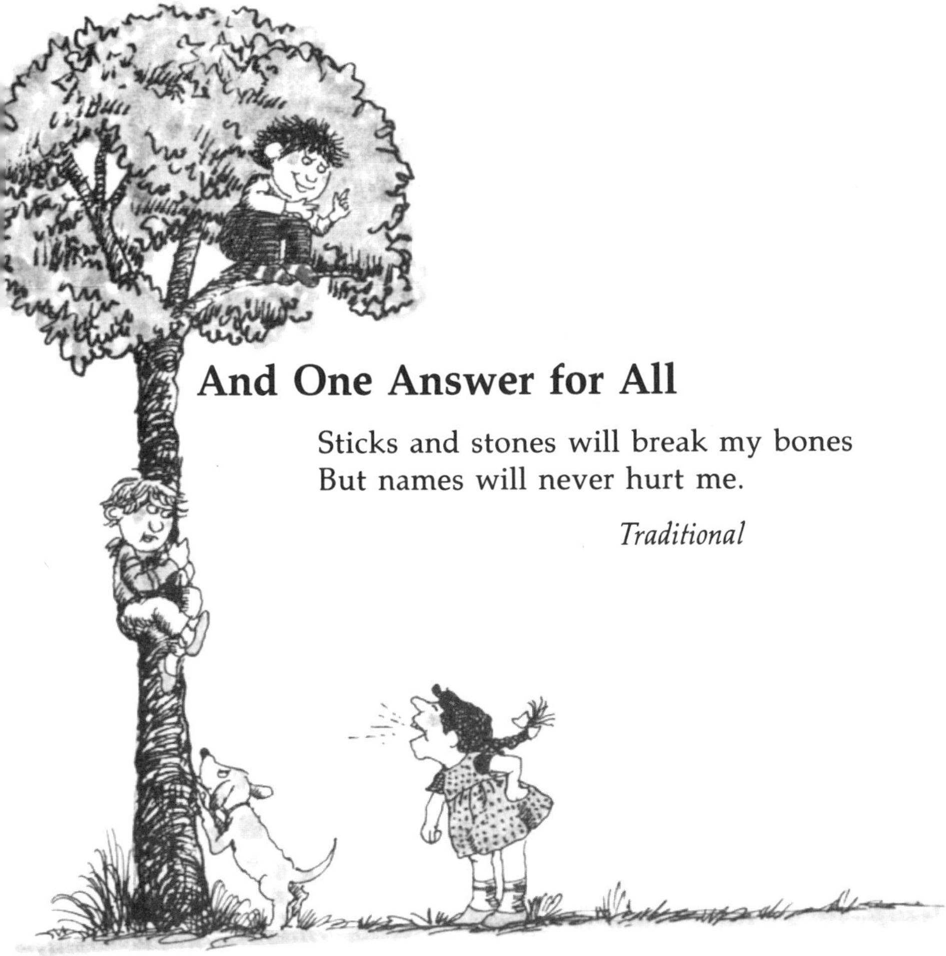

And One Answer for All

Sticks and stones will break my bones
But names will never hurt me.

Traditional

Jabberwocky

'Twas brillig, and the slithy toves
  Did gyre and gimble in the wabe:
All mimsy were the borogoves,
  And the mome raths outgrabe.

"Beware the Jabberwock, my son!
  The jaws that bite, the claws that catch!
Beware the Jubjub bird, and shun
  The frumious Bandersnatch!"

He took his vorpal sword in hand:
  Long time the manxome foe he sought—
So rested he by the Tumtum tree,
  And stood awhile in thought.

And, as in uffish thought he stood,
  The Jabberwock, with eyes of flame,
Came whiffling through the tulgey wood,
  And burbled as it came!

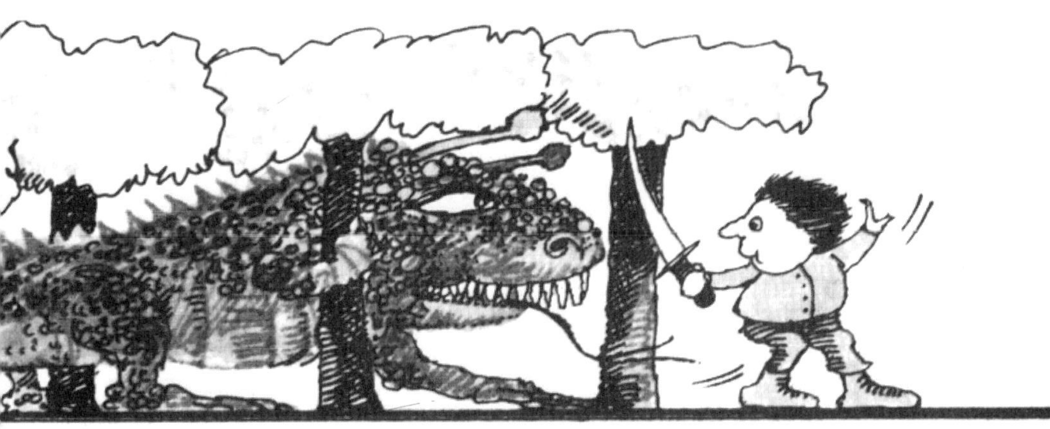

One, two! One, two! And through and through
The vorpal blade went snicker-snack!
He left it dead, and with its head
He went galumphing back.

"And hast though slain the Jabberwock?
Come to my arms, my beamish boy!
O frabjous day! Callooh! Callay!"
He chortled in his joy.

'Twas brillig, and the slithy toves
Did gyre and gimble in the wabe:
All mimsy were the borogoves,
And the mome raths outgrabe.

Lewis Carroll

Mairzy Doats

Mairzy doats and dozy doats
And liddle lamzy divey;
A kiddley divey too,
Wouldn't you?

(Mares eat oats and does eat oats
And little lambs eat ivy;
A kid'll eat ivy too,
Wouldn't you?)

Milton Drake, Al Hoffman,
and Jerry Livingston

Did You Eever, Iver, Over?

Did you eever, iver, over
In your leef, life, loaf
See the deevel, divel, dovel
Kiss his weef, wife, woaf?

No, I neever, niver, nover
In my leef, life, loaf,
Saw the deevel, divel, dovel
Kiss his weef, wife, woaf.

Traditional

Hand-Clapping Rhyme

Miss Lucy

Miss Lucy had a baby.
She named him Tiny Tim.
She put him in the bathtub
To see if he could swim.

He drank up all the water.
He ate up all the soap.
He tried to eat the bathtub,
But it wouldn't go down his throat.

Miss Lucy called the Doctor.
Miss Lucy called the Nurse.
Miss Lucy called the Lady
With the alligator purse.

In walked the Doctor.
In walked the Nurse.
In walked the Lady
With the alligator purse.

"Measles," said the Doctor.
"Chicken Pox," said the Nurse.
"Mumps," said the Lady
With the alligator purse.

Out walked the Doctor.
Out walked the Nurse.
Out walked the Lady
With the alligator purse.

Traditional

Mother Goose?

Twinkle, Twinkle, Little Bat

Twinkle, twinkle, little bat!
How I wonder what you're at!
Up above the world you fly,
Like a tea tray in the sky.

Lewis Carroll

Row, Row, Row Your Goat

Row, row, row your goat
Gently down the stream.
Merrily, merrily, merrily, merrily,
Life is just a scream.

Stephanie Calmenson

Little Miss Tuckett

Little Miss Tuckett
Sat on a bucket,
Eating some peaches and cream.
There came a grasshopper
And tried hard to stop her,
But she said, "Go way, or I'll scream."

Author Unknown

Say Dis with D's

The Penny in the Gum Slot

First say the poem this way:

I put the penny in the gum slot.
You saw the gum come down.
You get the wrapper.
I get the gum.
'Cause I put the penny in the gum slot.

Now say the same poem but begin every word with the letter D:

Die dut de denny din de dum dot.
Doo daw de dum dum down.
Doo det de dapper.
Die det de dum.
Dause die dut de denny din de dum dot.

Now say it again as fast as you can. Try it on a friend.

Author Unknown

4

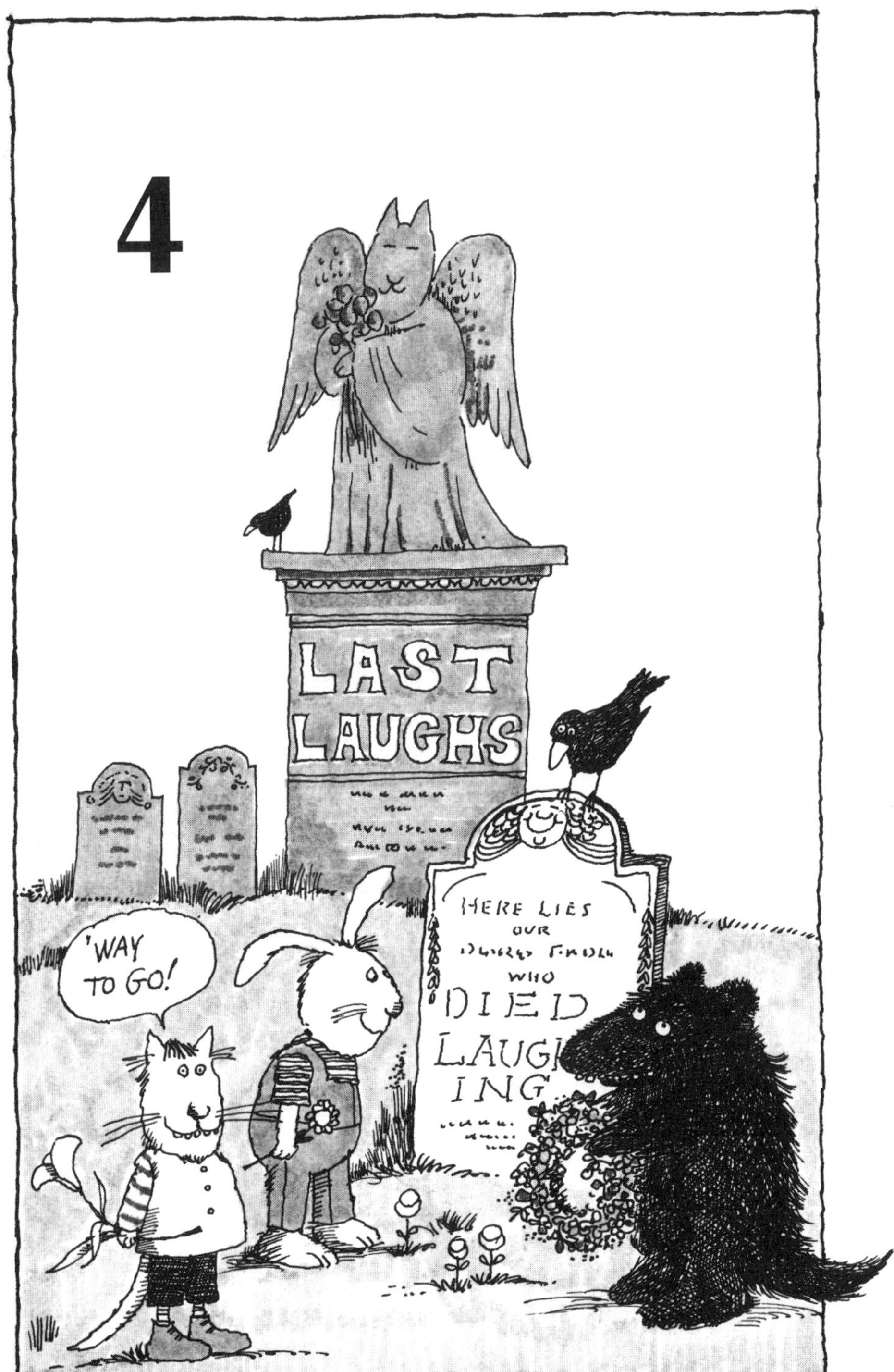

Newsbreaks

by Charles Keller

A boat carrying a shipment of Yo-Yos across the ocean sprang a leak and sank fifty times.

Because of a strike at the cemetery, gravedigging will be done by a skeleton crew.

Two hundred hares escaped from a rabbit farm; police are combing the area.

Best Sellers (Books You'll Never Read)

by Stephanie Calmenson

It's a Dog's Life by Ima Mongrel
Overcoming Your Fears by R. U. Yellow
The Private Eye's Handbook by Hugh Dunnit
How to Get Your Work Done Faster by Sheik Alleg
Weather Trends for the Future by Hugh Nose
True Love by I. M. Yaws
Beating the Blues by Watts D. Matter, M.D.
How to Weight-lift a Brick Building by Noah Kandoo
I Work for Peanuts by Ella Fant
By the Dawn's Early Light by Jose Canusi
Fix It, Dear Liza by Holin D. Buckit

Weather Report

by Judi Barrett

And now here is the weather report from the town of Chewandswallow, where residents eat whatever comes from the sky:

Lamb chops, becoming heavy at times, with occasional ketchup. Periods of peas and baked potatoes followed by gradual clearing, with a wonderful Jell-O setting in the west.

Tomorrow, cloudy with a chance of meatballs.

How to Get a Dog

by Delia Ephron

Tell your parents that you want a dog more than anything in this world. Promise that you'll take care of it. Cross your heart and hope to die. They won't have to do a thing. You'll walk it and feed it. Please. Please. Pretty-please. Pretty-please with sugar on top. Pretty-please with whipped cream and a cherry. Please, Mom, please. You are, too, old enough. When they say that you have to wait one more year, stamp your foot. Scream, "You never trust me; you never believe me. Why don't you trust me?"

Run to your room, slam the door, open the door, and yell, "It's not fair." Slam the door again. When your mother comes to your room, have the following conversation:

"That's enough," says she.

Say, "All right," as though it isn't.

"I said, 'That's enough.' "

"All I said was 'All right.' "

"It's not what you said, it's how you said it."

"Okay, Mom, but . . ."
and repeat entire scene from "I want a dog more than anything in the world" to "Why don't you trust me?" Convince her.

When your mother says that it's time to feed the dog, say, "Just a second." When she says it's time to walk the dog, say, "In a minute." After she reminds you again, tell her that you just want to watch the end of the TV show. Then take out the dog, complaining that it's so boring to walk it and besides you can't find the leash. Use your belt instead.

Each day, procrastinate and complain until your mother finds it easier to feed it and walk it herself.

How to Be the Perfect Host

by Pat Relf

You say you're thinking of having a party? Here are some tips you'll want to keep in mind:

The key to a successful party is *planning.* Your invitations must be sent to your guests well ahead of time. If the party is to be a formal affair, let your guests know what to wear by saying, "Make sure to wear an undershirt" or "Please paint your feet."

As your party draws near, make sure that your home is spanking clean. Remember: a place for everything and everything in its place, and when the place gets too crowded, there's always room under the bed. (By the way, you might want to hide that fungus farm of yours in your sock drawer. It will be safe there.)

Always take particular care in dressing. Your attire sets the tone for the evening. The perfectly groomed host knows that there's nothing like a tasteful anchovy bow tie to spice up an otherwise dull evening costume.

Thoughtful guests will bring their host a small gift, such as rubber bands or gravel. You will, of course, want to put the gravel in water at once. Don't forget to say, "Thank you very much. I just *love* gravel," even if you prefer mud or shredded paper.

Hang up your guests' coats neatly, taking special care not to wrinkle or dirty them. If an accident occurs, and you spill purple ink on a guest's coat, remember: salt, flour, concentrated orange juice, and a little more ink will remove the stain.

Proper introductions are essential to any successful social gathering. Be certain everyone at your party meets everyone else.

It is correct to introduce a four-headed monster in a clockwise direction, starting with the head closest to you. Upon being introduced yourself, say, "How do you do?" and shake hands. Shaking hands with a chicken poses a difficult problem. Our advice is to wing it.

You Can't Eat Peanuts in Church and Other Little-known Laws

by Barbara Seuling

All these are real *laws that are now or have been on the books!*

In Tahoe City, California, cowbells may not be worn by horses.

In San Francisco, you are forbidden by law to spit on your laundry.

In Idaho, you cannot buy a chicken after dark without the sheriff's permission.

In Wyoming, it is illegal to take a picture of a rabbit during January, February, March, or April—unless you have a license.

In New York, it is unlawful to disturb the occupant of a house by ringing the doorbell.

It is illegal to eat peanuts in church in Massachusetts.

Barbers in Hawaii are not permitted to lather the chins of their customers with a shaving brush.

In Baltimore, Maryland, it is against the law to mistreat an oyster.

The Frog Speaker

by Mike Thaler

The Doctor Is In

by Charles M. Schulz

Index

Joanna Cole is the author of many highly praised children's books, including *The Magic School Bus*™ series. She lives in Connecticut.

Stephanie Calmenson is the author of many popular books for children, including *The Principal's New Clothes*. She lives in New York.

Together, Cole and Calmenson have compiled several best-selling anthologies, including, for Doubleday, *The Read-Aloud Treasury, Ready . . . Set . . . Read!* and *The Laugh Book.*

Marylin Hafner has illustrated seventy books, including, in 1994, *And Then What, Chatterbox Jamie* and *Please Don't Feed the Guppies.* She is also the author and creator of the popular *Ladybug* magazine feature, "Molly and Emmett," now available as a book, *The Adventures of Molly and Emmett.* She lives in Massachusetts.